Shattered Resilience

JENNY HOUGHTON THOMAS

Copyright © 2024 Jenny Houghton
Thomas

All rights reserved.

ISBN: 979-8-9898351-0-2

DEDICATION

To my husband Daniel, my children Kurk, Kyle, Mya, Hannah, and Jack.
To my friends, family, and everyone throughout my life who has helped me along my journey.
And to all the kids who have gone through the broken system.

CONTENTS

1 THE UNRAVELING

Morning light filtered through my window, highlighting the small size of our town. We only had one stoplight and a single grocery store. Everyone knew each other, and it felt cozy, yet sometimes too close for comfort. Surrounding our town were farms as far as the eye could see, with fields of wheat and corn under the big Kansas sky. The town was quiet, except for the occasional distant sound of a tractor. This small town, with its simple life and routine, was a stark contrast to the complicated feelings I had been grappling with since mom got us away from my stepfather. That was two years ago, but time, it seemed, had lost its efficacy against the sediment of trauma that had settled in our minds.

The blanket around me felt warm and safe and I was reluctant to leave. It was the first morning in countless days where my nightmares hadn't ushered me into consciousness—a small mercy. The stuffed bear from my childhood gazed at me with button eyes, a mute witness to the metamorphosis of the girl who once played in the sunshine without the threat of storms.

Stepping onto the cold floor, I was reminded that not all things were warm in this newfound peace. The ground felt solid, and unyielding, a quick reminder of the stability we had fought so hard to reclaim. The walls of my room, freshly painted in a hopeful hue of yellow, held no trace of our history. They stood silent, guarding the secrets of a past that bled into our present.

I moved quietly through the house, a habit born from the need to avoid the mines of my stepfather's temper. Each step was measured, a soft tread on the path that wound through this semblance of normalcy we were still learning to navigate.

As I walked through the hallway, I took note of the gallery of my family's aspirations, frames capturing smiles that were often rehearsed, moments meticulously curated to overwrite the memories we wished to forget. My mother's face, beaming in photographs, belied the nights I heard her muffled sobs through the walls. Lily's laughter, forever captured in still life, couldn't quite mask the times it was silenced by fear. Henry's playful poses couldn't erase the memory of his withdrawn silences, and John's shielding stance couldn't make me forget the times he was powerless to protect us.

Entering the kitchen, the aroma of coffee and the sizzle of frying eggs promised that semblance of normalcy I often heard my mother speak of. Mom was the epitome of resilience and moved with a grace that defied the weight I knew she carried. She was the cornerstone of our family. Her newly permed, short brown hair and large glasses framed a face marked by a steadfast devotion to us, her children, surpassing what one might typically expect from a mother. Her smile was the daybreak we all leaned towards, but I wondered if she, like me, felt the night was never quite vanquished.

"Morning, Sarah," she said, her voice a melody of warmth as she pulled me into her embrace.

"Morning, Mom," I responded, my voice betraying none of the turmoil that churned within. Her hugs temporarily made me feel safe, but my demons had learned to scale those walls.

The kitchen table was an island where my siblings cast away the remnants of our shared tempest. Lily, with her vibrant energy and bouncing blonde curls, danced around the room, her youth a rebuke to the shadows that still clung to me. Henry, my younger brother, injected levity into the morning with his playful antics. His resilience, shaped by early years marred by surgeries for his club foot, never ceased to amaze me. And John, three years older than me, recently ditched his thick glasses for contacts, embodying his silent transition into a more adult role, especially noticeable since he started a new after-school job at the local pizzeria.

 We gathered around the table, a ritual of togetherness that felt both healing and alienating. They all talked about how school was going, upcoming birthday parties they were invited to, and weekend plans. Their voices weaving a tapestry of life moving forward as I watched them, trying to include myself but failing. I was an observer in my own life.

"How's the new job, John?" Mom asked, her voice a lighthouse guiding us through the fog of unspoken pain.

"It's good, keeping me busy," John replied, his eyes briefly meeting mine, sharing a sliver of the burden we both carried.

Lily continued to chatter about school, her spirit untamed by the darkness that had once threatened to extinguish it. Henry, not to be outdone, regaled us with tales of his latest adventures, his animated gestures painting pictures in the air.

I tried to join in, to let their joy seep into the cracks

of my fractured self, but it was like watching life through a glass—visible, yet untouchable. I laughed when it was expected, and nodded at the right moments, but it was a performance and a role I had perfected.

The clock ticked on, indifferent to my stagnation. The world had continued to spin, and they had spun with it, finding their rhythm in the dance of healing. But I remained out of step, my movements discordant with the melody of recovery they had composed.

As breakfast came to an end, the laughter fading into the hum of the day, I felt a heavy pressure in my chest. They were moving on, each step taking them further from the ruins of our past. I wondered if I would ever find the strength to join them in the light, or if I was destined to be an eternal resident of the dusk, forever reaching for a dawn that was just beyond my grasp.

I carried my plate to the sink, my movements automatic and the clink of the dishes interrupting my scattered thoughts. I closed my eyes and allowed my mind to wander as the warm water and soap suds created a miniature whirlpool beneath me.

"Sarah, you okay?" John's voice cut through the fog, pulling me back to the present.

I met his gaze, a mirror reflecting back my own uncertainty. "I'm getting there," I lied, the words a fragile bridge over an expanse I was still mapping.

He nodded, the unspoken understanding between us was a tether that kept me anchored. In his eyes, I found a reflection of my own resilience, a fractured resilience, but resilience nonetheless. And in that moment, I allowed myself to believe that maybe, possibly, the path to healing wasn't a solitary trek. Perhaps it was a journey we could navigate together, as a family, each step a testament to the enduring strength of our bond.

The breakfast dishes clinked softly as I placed them in the rack to dry, the sound echoing slightly in the quiet aftermath of our morning congregation. My movements were methodical, a dance of routine that I performed with a precision that belied the chaos churning underneath. The soap suds, iridescent and fleeting, swirled down the drain, carrying with them a metaphor for the transient calm that seemed to elude my grasp.

I glanced out the kitchen window, the glass framing a world that seemed both intimately familiar and hopelessly foreign. The garden, once a jungle of untamed weeds, now bore the fruits of John's labor—a testament to our collective effort to cultivate beauty from neglect. The flowers, a riot of color against the green, swayed gently in the breeze, each bloom was a silent cheerleader for resilience.

While my fingers traced the rim of the porcelain sink, I let my gaze drift to the small kitchen table, its surface still littered with the remnants of our meal—the crumpled napkins, the stray crumbs, the empty chairs that seemed to hold the afterimage of my family's presence.

The silence was a canvas, and upon it, the faintest sounds painted a picture of domestic tranquility: the distant hum of a lawnmower, the soft whisper of the breeze through the open window, the rhythmic ticking of the wall clock. Yet, beneath the veneer of peace, the canvas was marred by the smudges of past turmoil, the darker colors of our shared history bleeding through.

I caught my distorted reflection in the polished chrome of the toaster. It was a fitting metaphor for how I saw myself—warped by the memories of darker days, struggling to fit into the frame of who I was expected to become. I turned away, unwilling to confront the stranger who looked back at me.

Upstairs, the sound of Lily's music trickled down, a cascade of pop melodies that spoke of teenage dreams and carefree hearts. It was a language I had once been fluent in, but now the words and beats seemed to pass through me, leaving no impression. I wondered if the music masked her own struggles or if she had truly managed to distance herself from the echoes of our past.

Henry's laughter bubbled up from the living room, the soundtrack to the morning cartoons he still clung to, a vestige of childhood innocence that he wasn't ready to relinquish. I envied him that anchor, that tether to a simpler time when the monsters were on the screen and not in our lives.

I felt John's presence before I saw him, his quiet strength a constant undercurrent in the flow of our family's dynamics. He leaned against the doorframe, his eyes carrying the wisdom of one who has seen too much, yet still manages to find a way to look ahead. Something I have always envied about him.

"You're deep in thought," he observed, crossing the room to stand beside me.

"Just reflecting," I admitted, turning to meet his steady gaze.

He nodded, understanding the unspoken words that lingered between us. "You know, sometimes I think we're like this house," he mused, gesturing to the walls that surrounded us. "We've got our cracks and creaks, and we've weathered some serious storms. But we're still standing. We're still here."

His analogy brought a small smile to my lips, a rare and genuine upturn that felt like a balm to my weary spirit. "We're a little worse for wear, though," I added.

"Maybe," he conceded, "but that just adds to our character. Makes us who we are."

I pondered his words, the idea that our trials had shaped us, molded us into a family with a foundation stronger for all the fractures it had endured. It was a comforting thought, one that offered a glimmer of hope in the relentless dusk of my doubts.

"Come on," John said gently, breaking into my reverie. "Let's go join the living."

I allowed myself to be led into the living room, where the sunlight spilled onto the carpet in lazy beams, where Henry's laughter still rang out, and Lily's music still played. And for a moment, just a fleeting moment, I felt the weight within me lighten, the shadows recede, and the warmth of my family's love seep into the cold places in my heart.

As I settled onto the couch, letting the familiarity of the moment wrap around me, I realized that healing wasn't a solitary journey—it was a path we walked together, each of us a beacon for the others when the way grew dark. And perhaps, in this shared journey, I would find the strength to step fully into the light and let go of the dusk that had become my solace.

2 BATTLES WITHIN

The halls of Skyfield Middle School were packed as
I walked through them that morning. The loud
sound of lockers closing rang in my ears, making
me feel the mess inside my head even more. I got to
my seat just as the second bell rang, signaling the
start of another long day.

Mrs. Keller was talking about algebra, but I could
barely hear her with all the thoughts running
through my mind. Everyone groaned when she
brought it up. I tried to pay attention to the
whiteboard, but the numbers and equations looked
too complicated for me to understand right now.

I used to be really good at math, solving problems
easily. But that feels like a long time ago, before I
started having all these troubled thoughts. Now,
when I look at numbers, they just seem mixed up
and confusing, like a puzzle I can't figure out.

A nudge at my elbow brought me back, and I turned
to see Ben, his brow creased in concern. "You're

spacing out again, Sarah. You sure you're okay?" he whispered, his voice a lifeline thrown into the turbulent sea of my thoughts.

Ben and I had been friends since the 5th grade when we had found the same trees to walk through, killing time during recess. Ben was bullied by the other boys for being so tiny and having thick glasses and I liked to be away from the other girls who were starting to talk too much about boys.

I forced my lips to curve in the semblance of a smile—a smile I'd mastered in the art of false reassurances. "Just didn't sleep well," I lied smoothly. "I'll catch up."

The real problem was that I wasn't just missing sleep. It was the nightmares that stuck in my mind. They twisted through my dreams like they knew what they were doing, leaving me feeling scared and confused when I woke up.

The day dragged on, and each class felt like a challenge. I struggled to recall dates in history, avoided gym class activities that made me feel out of touch with my body and tried to ignore my friends' concerns about the dimming light they saw in my eyes.

At lunch, I sat with my friends but felt out of place. Their laughter was overwhelming compared to the quiet turmoil in my mind. I barely ate, each mouthful reminding me how different I felt from everyone else. I heard their conversations like a faint noise in the background, sometimes a word or phrase catching my attention and breaking through my wall of thoughts.

"Sarah's been quiet today," I overheard someone murmur, a statement that rippled through the table's conversation with the subtlety of a stone breaking the surface of a still pond.

"I'm just not hungry," I mumbled when the collective gaze of the group settled on me, probing, questioning. Their concern was a warm blanket I wanted to shrug off, suffocated by the weight of its expectation to be okay.

I finally heard the last bell and was ready to leave. Quickly, I got my bag from my locker and made my way through the crowded hallway. Stepping outside, the bright sunlight made me feel exposed, as if everyone could see through my façade of pretending to be okay.

Standing at the edge of the school, it felt like I was on the border of two different worlds. Inside, I felt a storm of emotions ready to burst. I was trying so hard to keep everything under control, but I was scared it might all fall apart.

But not today. Today, I still had control over how I appeared to others, holding back my inner turmoil. With a deep breath that seemed both vital and final, I moved on, facing yet another invisible struggle within myself.

As long as I stayed away from a certain group of kids, I had mastered going unnoticed at school, careful with every move and gesture. But keeping up this act was tiring, leaving me feeling drained inside. My friends seemed like an audience watching me, expecting me to act a certain way. But underneath it all, I was struggling, weighed down by problems that no one else could see.

My friendship with Emily, who I've known since I was little, used to be a safe place for me. But now, it's like looking in a mirror and not recognizing myself. Emily tries to help and really cares, but her words can't seem to reach me. It's like I'm just slipping away, unable to connect or feel understood or supported.

Ben, with his easy smile and earnest eyes, had stood by me through the ups and downs. But now, our friendship feels shaky, like it's on the edge of falling apart because I'm so lost in my own thoughts. I see him looking at me sometimes, full of questions I'm not ready to answer. I know he wants to help, but I'm scared to lean on him. I worry that if I do, I might pull him down with me into my troubles.

The walk through the neighborhood was a journey through a landscape that had grown foreign. The houses, that once felt friendly, now seemed distant, mirroring my own feelings of isolation. Arriving home, I was met by my mother and siblings who carried on like nothing was wrong. Our conversations were a delicate dance around the truth, a truth that I cloaked in half-truths and deflections.

Dinner was a quiet affair, with only the sounds of our forks and knives scaping against plates. My mom and older brother exchanged glances over the rim of their glasses, their silent conversation a language of worry I had come to understand all too well.

"School was fine," I would offer to the inquiring looks, the same lie repackaged in different words, served alongside the evening meal.

Retreating to my room, I was greeted by the relics of a time when my biggest concern was the next math test, not the maze of my own psyche. The walls were adorned with the artifacts of my former self — posters of bands that sang of love and heartache, their words now sounding like distant echoes of a life I could only half-remember.

As night wrapped its arms around the house, I lay in bed, staring at the ceiling where shadows played out scenes from a life that I felt I was observing from the outside. The soft glow of my alarm clock was the only light in the dark, like a lighthouse guiding ships too far gone from shore. Sleep was a reluctant visitor that night, stealing into my consciousness only to lead me through a twisted wonderland where memories and monsters danced together.

The question whispered in the dark, a hiss that slithered into my thoughts — how much longer could I bear this? Yet, despite everything, I clung to the remnants of hope. In the quiet predawn hours, I resolved to continue the fight. Inside all the chaos in my mind, I found a bit of peace and held on to it believing things would get better.

Each new day was a challenge, and I put on my act of being normal. I got ready, trying hard to keep my inner chaos under control.

My days became a cycle of pretending and struggling. I acted like everything was fine, hiding my real feelings behind smiles and polite responses. But inside, I was fighting hard, each day a struggle for my inner peace.

Every morning, I hoped that this might be the day when things would start to look up, when light would be a sign of good things, not bad. With each sunrise, I held on to the hope that one day, peace wouldn't be far away, but right where I was.

3 NO ESCAPE

The clock's ticking matched my restlessness, each sound bringing me closer to a night without peaceful sleep. I lay in bed, feeling empty, as the remnants of another day slipped through the window, the moonlight casting a pale glow on the walls of my room.

I could feel the darkness waiting for me, just beyond the veil of wakefulness, a kingdom of nightmares holding the memories of my past—vivid, cruel, and relentless. I closed my eyes, and the familiar dread settled in, a thick fog obscuring the line between the past and the present.

The dreams came as they always did, unbidden and savage. I was back there, in the room where innocence was a feeble light extinguished too soon. His shadow loomed over me, the scent of alcohol heavy in the air, a prelude to the storm. I could feel his hands, rough and demanding, a violation of my being that time refused to erase.

I woke up suddenly, the echo of a silent scream trapped in my throat. The sheets were tangled around me, a shroud of sweat and fear. My breath came in ragged gasps, a desperate rhythm as I fought to anchor myself to reality.

"Just a dream," I whispered into the darkness, a mantra that lost its power with each passing night.

The room felt smaller, the walls inching closer, a prison of my own making. I needed an escape, a breach in the fortress I had built around myself. The urge was sudden, a whisper of temptation that promised relief.

I got out of my bed, my movements ghostly as I drifted to the dresser. The blade was hidden beneath a pile of forgotten trinkets, its surface cold and indifferent. My hand trembled as I held it, the metal a false friend that offered a momentary respite from the pain within.

A small act, a line drawn across the skin, and the world narrowed to a single point of focus. It was a release, a way to control the chaos, to feel something—anything—other than the numbness that had become my constant companion.

The sting was sharp, a punctuation to the dull ache in my soul. I watched, detached, as the blood welled up, a stark contrast to the paleness of my skin. It was a moment of clarity, a fleeting sense of dominion over my own flesh, but it was a victory tainted with shame.

I bandaged the wound with mechanical precision, a routine that I had perfected in secret. The pain lingered, a reminder of my weakness, of the depths to which I had sunk in my silent battle.

The house was quiet as I made my way downstairs, the floorboards creaking underfoot, a betrayal of my nocturnal unrest. The kitchen was shrouded in shadows, the countertops bathed in the soft light of the moon filtering through the blinds.

I knew where she kept it, the cabinet above the fridge, a cache of bottles holding liquid forgetfulness. It was an unspoken understanding, the lock on the door a feeble deterrent, a symbol rather than a safeguard.

The alcohol burned as it went down, a fire that ignited my insides, a warmth that spread through my chest. I welcomed it, the oblivion it promised, a respite from the relentless siege of memories.

I didn't hear her until it was too late, her voice a shard of ice that cut through the haze.

"Sarah, what are you doing?"

I turned to face my mother, her features drawn in a

mixture of confusion and dawning horror. The bottle dangled from my fingertips, an accusation that hung in the space between us.

"Nothing," I lied, the word a stone that sank in the silence.

"This isn't nothing," she said softly, taking a step closer. Her eyes searched mine, looking for the daughter she knew, but finding instead a stranger gazing back at her through a veil of pain.

"Why, Sarah?" Her voice cracked, a fissure in the facade of strength she wore like armor.

I wanted to tell her everything, to unload the burden that had become too heavy to bear alone. But the words were trapped, caged behind a wall of fear and shame.

"I just wanted to forget," I admitted, the truth a whisper that seemed to echo in the stillness of the kitchen.

She took the bottle from me, her touch gentle, as though she was afraid that I would shatter. "This isn't the way," she said, her eyes glistening with unshed tears. "We'll find another way."

But as she held me, I felt the warmth of her embrace as a distant echo, a comfort I could see and touch but not quite accept into the numbness that filled me. Her arms wrapped around my shoulders, trying to offer comfort in my deep sadness. But I still felt lost,, unable to reconcile the person I had become with the daughter she held.

"We'll get through this," she murmured, her voice steady, a guiding light in the chaos of my life. But her words, meant to soothe, struggled to reach me.

The silence that followed was filled with the weight of words unsaid. There was a tense feeling in the air between us, full of our shared hurt. Her hand, trembling slightly, brushed the damp strands of hair from my face—a gesture so full of the maternal love I remembered from childhood, from before the world had revealed its true, unforgiving nature.

I wanted to believe her—I wanted to believe in the possibility of a life reclaimed from the wreckage. Yet belief was a fragile thing, and I couldn't see past what I was going through at that moment.

The kitchen, once a stage for family gatherings and whispered midnight confessions, now felt like a tribunal. Each appliance, each piece of furniture, bore witness to my unraveling. The refrigerator hummed a chant for the peace we once knew, the countertops gleamed coldly under the moonlight, and the tiles under my feet were the cold bars of a cell I had constructed, brick by brick, with every unspoken secret and suppressed emotion.

I broke away from her embrace, a quiet apology in the motion. The need for solitude was a gnawing ache, the only clarity in the chaos of my thoughts. I could feel her gaze on my back as I ascended the staircase, each step a heavy drumbeat in the quiet house.

My room was both a sanctuary and a prison. The walls held the remnants of a past self—posters of bands whose lyrics had once been anthems to my innocence. Now, they were just paper and ink, their messages as distant as the stars outside my window.

I closed the door with a soft click, the sound of a closing chapter. My reflection in the mirror stared back at me, the familiar contours of my face now a map of the tumultuous journey I had undertaken. The eyes that looked back at me held a reservoir of silent screams, each one echoing in the hollows of my self-imposed exile.

The blade called to me again, a siren song that promised the paradoxical relief of pain over numbness, of physical sensation over the oppressive emptiness. It was a craving, a whisper in my blood that spoke of release, of control in a life that felt increasingly beyond my command.

But as I reached for it, a sliver of moonlight caught the edge of the metal, casting a long, ominous shadow across the floor. It was the shadow of a choice, a crossroads where each path led further into darkness. The temporary relief I felt was just an illusion, like a mirage in the desert, leaving me even more empty each time I turned to it.

I set the blade down, a small victory over the impulse, and wrapped my arms around myself, an embrace that was both an admission of vulnerability and a show of strength. I was alone, utterly alone in that moment, with nothing but the beat of my heart and the rise and fall of my chest to affirm that I was still alive, that I still existed beyond the pain.

The night stretched on, an expanse of time that offered no solace. In the darkness, I traced the arc of my journey, from the girl who danced in the sunlight to the stranger in the mirror. Each moment was a brushstroke on the canvas of my life, a life that had become a shadowy mixture of light and dark, of hope and despair.

As the first hints of dawn crept across the sky, painting it in the pale hues of morning, I remained awake, a sentinel in the silent hours. The war within me raged on, but with the new day came the faintest glimmer of hope, a hope that maybe, just maybe, the path to dawn lay in the courage to face the coming light.

4 SHATTERED

The world outside was dark, but inside, I was no stranger to the shadows that clung to the corners of my room. Each night was longer than the last, a relentless tide of sleeplessness and dread. I stared at the ceiling, tracing the patterns of the stucco with tired eyes, finding shapes in the texture that resembled the chaos within me.

My skin itched with a familiar burn, a yearning for the sharp bite of the blade I had hidden away. It was a call for relief, a physical pain to drown out the emotional torture that kept me ensnared in its unforgiving grip. I resisted, but the bottle of vodka, half-empty and carelessly capped, beckoned from downstairs—a siren's call.

The silence of the night was broken by a whimper, a soft sound of distress that seemed loud in the stillness. I turned my head, listening harder. There it was again—a small, scared sound that I knew all too well. It was my little sister, Lily.

I shuffled from my bed, my limbs heavy, my movements sluggish, as if I were wading through water. The hallway seemed longer than normal, the faint light from the moon casting long, twisted shadows across the floor, like dark fingers reaching out for me.

Lily's room was cracked open, a sliver of darkness against the dimly lit corridor. The whimpers grew louder as I approached, and I pushed the door open to see her tangled in her sheets, her small body thrashing as if to fend off an unseen attacker.

"No," she mumbled, her voice thick with fear. "Please, stop it."

My heart clenched. The words were a chilling echo of my own pleas, a mirror reflecting the past that continued to haunt us both. I moved to her side, reaching out to gently shake her awake.

"Lily," I whispered. "It's just a dream. You're safe."

Her eyes fluttered open, large and brimming with tears, her gaze unfocused as she struggled to separate the nightmare from reality.

"Why does he keep coming back?" she asked, her voice a fragile thread of sound.

I pulled her into my arms, her small frame fitting easily against mine. "He's gone, Lily. He can't hurt us anymore," I said, the lie bitter on my tongue. Because he was still here, wasn't he? In our minds, in our dreams, he was as present as the night around us.

I held her until her breathing evened out, until the tremors that shook her body subsided. She fell back into a restless sleep, and I tucked the covers around her protectively. The anger simmered in me—a fierce, protective rage that had no outlet, no target. It burned hotter with every one of Lily's shaky breaths.

The anger stayed with me as I walked to school the next day. It was a heavy chain around my neck, a weight that I carried in the pit of my stomach. My steps were a march, a soldier going to war against an enemy that was my own mind.

School felt like a battleground, the hallways full of whispers and sidelong glances. I was like a shadow that drifted through the everyday lives of those around me. They noticed. Of course, they noticed. How could they not when I wore my pain like a second skin?

"Ghost girl," they called me. "Freak."

The names were like stones thrown at my back, each one a pinpoint of pain that I added to the collection I carried. I kept walking, my head down, my fists clenched at my sides.

It was in the cafeteria where the dam finally broke. A group of them, led by Jessica Miller, a girl with a mean streak as wide as her smile, cornered me.

"Why so quiet, Sarah?" she taunted, her voice dripping with false sweetness. "Cat got your tongue, or is it just that no one cares to listen to what you have to say?"

The others laughed, a cruel, harsh sound that bounced off the walls and filled the space around us. I felt the heat rise in my cheeks, the anger that had simmered now boiling over.

"Leave me alone," I said, my voice low, a warning growl that they either didn't hear or chose to ignore.

"What's wrong? Gonna cry? Go on, run away like you always do," Jessica sneered, stepping closer, her face inches from mine.

I didn't run. Instead, I lashed out, my hand moving of its own accord. There was a moment of shock, a split second where the world paused, and then chaos erupted.

The fight was brief, a flurry of limbs and shouted curse words. It ended with us both on the ground, me on top, my fist raised, her face a canvas of fear and surprise. It took two teachers to pull me off of her, to pry my fingers from the collar of her shirt.

They dragged me away, the murmurs of the crowd a dull roar in my ears. I was numb, removed from the moment as if watching it happen to someone else.

In the principal's office, I sat, a hollow shell filled with roiling emotions, as accusations were thrown and punishment decided. Suspension. It was a word that meant little to me, a consequence that held no weight against the gravity of my internal struggle.

My mother's face when she came to collect me was a mask of disappointment and confusion. "What happened?" she asked, her voice breaking on the words.

I couldn't answer. How could I explain the unexplainable? How could I articulate the rage, the fear, the despair that had become my frequent companions?

The drive home was shrouded in a thick veil of silence, broken only by the occasional shuffling of my mother's hands on the steering wheel. The disappointment radiating from her was palpable, a tangible force that filled the cramped space of the car.

"How could you let it go this far, Sarah?" Her voice quivered with a cocktail of emotions: disbelief, sorrow, frustration.

I stared out the window, the world outside a blur of colors that I couldn't quite bring into focus. I felt her eyes on me, waiting, hoping for an explanation I couldn't give. "I don't know," I murmured, the words hollow, tasting of defeat.

Her sigh was heavy, laden with the weight of our shared burdens. "This isn't you, Sarah. This anger... this violence. It's not you."

But she was wrong. It was me—this new version of myself that I didn't recognize, that I couldn't control. The anger was a living thing inside me, a beast that had been quietly growing, feeding on the scraps of my brokenness.

At home, the air felt charged, like the static before a storm. Lily's eyes darted to me, then away, a scared rabbit in the presence of a predator. I hated that look. I hated what I had done to cause it.

The rebellion at school had been a release valve, but now, back in the supposed sanctuary of my home, the pressure was building again, the walls closing in. I snapped at my little brother when he asked if I was okay, my words a whip that left invisible welts.

Dinner was filled with unspoken words and sidelong glances. My fork was heavy in my hand, each bite of food seemed to take more effort than it should have needed. My mother's attempts at conversation were met with quick responses or, worse, an icy silence.

In my room, the guilt gnawed at me. I sat on my bed, the chaos of my mind a stark contrast to the neatly ordered space. The guilt was a new companion, joining the ranks of the other dark entities that kept me company. It whispered to me of the pain I was causing, of the collateral damage in this war I was waging with myself.

The mirror on the wall caught my reflection, and I stared into the eyes of the stranger there. I saw the transformation, the hardening of my gaze, the set of my jaw. I was morphing into someone else, someone I didn't want to be.

Lily's laughter, once a melody, now sounded like a tune from another life. I could hear her through the walls, a reminder of what was at stake, of what I stood to lose.

I wanted to scream, to tear down the walls, to shatter the mirror—anything to break free from the prison of my own making. But instead, I sat, immobilized by my own fears, by the realization that I was the architect of my despair.

The night offered no comfort, no advice—just the

silent company of the moon and stars, witnesses to my internal catastrophe. I lay back on the bed, the darkness enveloping me, a cloak woven from the threads of my unraveling psyche.

"How long can I endure?" I whispered to the shadows. No answer came, just the echo of my own voice, a ghost in the darkness.

The war within raged on, a relentless siege with no end in sight. And as I closed my eyes, willing sleep to come, my mother called us into the living room. She stood by the fireplace, a silent sentinel, her face etched with worry. Lily and the boys were already seated, their expressions a mix of concern and curiosity. I lingered in the doorway, hesitant to join the semicircle of solemn faces.

"Sarah, please sit down. We need to talk as a family," my mother's voice was steady, but I could hear the tremor of concern beneath her words.

I complied, folding into the armchair furthest from the group, my arms crossed defensively. Her eyes met mine, holding a plea for understanding. "We're all worried about you," she began, her gaze sweeping over my siblings who nodded their agreement.

John's voice was the first to break the silence that followed. "What's going on with you, Sarah? You're not... you're not yourself lately."

Lily's small hand found mine, her touch tentative. "You scare me sometimes," she whispered, the admission a physical blow to my already fragile state.

The room spun with their words, each one laden with the weight of their love and fear for me. "I'm fine," the lie was automatic, but even to my own ears, it sounded hollow.

Mom shook her head, a lock of hair falling across her eyes. "Getting into fights, coming home with bruises, and now... now this." She gestured helplessly around the room. "This isn't fine, Sarah. We think... I think it's time to get some help."

The word 'help' hung in the air, a solution so simple yet so complex. I recoiled at the suggestion, the walls I had built to keep them out reinforcing themselves. "I don't need help," I snapped, the words sharp, a shield raised against their concern.

"But you do, Sarah. We can't pretend everything is normal when it's not," my mother persisted, her voice cracking with emotion.

I stood abruptly, the chair scraping against the wood floor. "This is normal for me! Can't you see that?" I shouted, my voice a wild thing, untamed and desperate.

The confrontation left us all breathless, the chasm between us widening with every word spoken. In the end, I fled the room, the house, the suffocating embrace of my family's good intentions.

That night, I sought solace in the reckless abandon of vandalism, the thrill of destruction a temporary balm for the pain. But as I stood, spray can in hand, the fumes mingling with the cool night air, a clarity pierced the fog of my anger. I knew where I would find my relief.

As I walked toward the bridge above the river that ran through town, I could feel the sting of tears welling in my eyes. I knew this was the end of my suffering but I couldn't help but think of my baby sister and who would help her when she woke from her nightmares.

Upon reaching the bridge, I shook the thought from my head, climbed over the railing, and without another thought, I leaped into the cold, unforgiving water below.

5 A NEW DAWN

Cold water enveloped me, a chilling embrace that numbed not just my skin but my soul. The darkness of the river was a mirror to the one I had been living in for far too long. But as I let go, ready to sink into the abyss, a force stronger than the current pulled me back to the surface.

"Sarah! Hold on!" John's voice was a distant echo, but his arms around me were real and strong. His grasp was desperate, terrified, as he dragged me out of the water and onto the riverbank.

Lying there, coughing and gasping, the reality of what I had almost done hit me like a physical blow. John was on his phone, voice shaky as he called for an ambulance. "It's going to be okay, Sarah. Just stay with me," he kept repeating, his words a lifeline I wasn't sure I deserved.

The ambulance arrived in a blur of lights and sounds. Paramedics swarmed around me, their voices calm and professional, a stark contrast to the chaos within me. As they lifted me onto a stretcher, my eyes locked with John's. The relief and fear in his eyes were a reflection of my own turmoil.

The hospital was a flurry of activity. Nurses and doctors worked over me, their faces masks of concentration. I was a spectator in my own drama, detached, watching the scene unfold as if it were happening to someone else.

Over the next few days, as my physical strength returned, the emotional weight of my actions began to press down on me. Lying in the sterile hospital bed, I felt exposed, both to the clinical lights and to the scrutiny of those who came to visit.

My family walked on eggshells around me, their concern wrapped in layers of confusion and hurt. Mom tried to hide her tears, but I saw them. Lily's visits were short, her usual vibrancy dimmed by the shadows in my room.

John's visits were the hardest. He didn't say much, but he didn't need to. His presence was a silent reminder of what I had almost taken from them. We were a family shattered, each trying to navigate the debris of my actions.

"I'm sorry," I whispered during one of his visits, the

words inadequate to express the depth of my regret.

John just nodded, his hand finding mine. "We're just glad you're still here, Sarah. That's all that matters."

But was it? In the quiet hours of the night, as I lay awake listening to the sounds of the hospital, I battled with my own thoughts. Relief at being alive warred with resentment over the failure of my plan. I felt trapped in a cycle of guilt and despair, each emotion feeding the other.

The hardest part was the uncertainty - not knowing how to move forward, how to mend the fractures I had caused. The hospital room, with its antiseptic smell and the constant beeping of machines, became a prison, a place where I was forced to confront the reality of my existence.

As the days passed, the initial shock of my situation gave way to a deep-seated fear of what was to come. The future was a blank canvas, but where I once saw potential, I now saw only a void.

My family's visits became a routine, a dance of awkward conversations and unspoken questions. We were all grappling in our own way, trying to find a new normal in the aftermath of my near-fatal decision.

The day of my discharge arrived, and with it, a complex mix of emotions. There was a part of me that longed for the familiarity of my own bed, the comfort of my room. But there was also a part that dreaded leaving the safety of the hospital, where my responsibilities were limited to physical recovery.

"Sarah, you're ready to go," the nurse said with a gentle smile, handing me a small bag with my belongings. Her voice was soft, but it couldn't mask the underlying note of formality that reminded me I was just another patient in her care.

I nodded, clutching the bag to my chest. The simple act of holding something of my own felt strangely grounding. As I stepped out of the room, I glanced back, half-expecting the bed and its neatly tucked sheets to hold some part of me I was leaving behind. But it was just an empty bed in an empty room.

Walking through the hospital corridors, I felt the weight of every step. Relief at being alive was tangled with embarrassment and anger over my failed attempt to end it all. I was stepping back into a world I wasn't sure I knew how to navigate anymore.

The car ride to the mental health facility was a quiet journey. My mother, who insisted on accompanying me, kept stealing glances in my direction, her eyes brimming with unspoken questions and worries.

As we pulled up to the state hospital, a chill ran down my spine. The building loomed large and foreboding, its stark exterior a harsh reminder of why I was here. I could hear distant shouts, the sounds of distress that resonated with the turmoil inside me.

Stepping inside, the atmosphere was thick with tension. I saw a young boy, no older than me, being restrained by security guards as he screamed for his mother. The sight sent a shiver through me, mirroring the scream that had been lodged in my own throat for far too long.

My mother squeezed my hand, her own shaking slightly. "Sarah, it's going to be okay," she whispered, more to herself than to me.

I wanted to believe her, but the fear and uncertainty that clutched at me were overwhelming. This place, with its echoes of pain and struggle, felt like a mirror reflecting the darkest parts of myself.

As we walked to the admissions room, the stares of other patients followed me, their gazes piercing through my already fragile armor. I was an intruder in their world, yet another lost soul seeking refuge from the chaos of her mind.

The admissions process was a blur of forms and questions, each one a reminder that I was no longer just Sarah, but a patient, a case to be managed and treated. When my mother finally left, her parting words were a mix of reassurance and sorrow, leaving me standing at the threshold of this new chapter in my life.

"Everything is going to be okay, Sarah. I love you so much and just need you to get better."

The first night in the facility was the longest night of my life. My room was tiny and uninviting, the bed and its linens institutional and unwelcoming. The sounds of the facility were a constant backdrop – the distant cries, the murmur of voices, the occasional clatter of someone walking down the hall.

Lying in bed, I was alone with my thoughts, which were as loud as the noises that permeated the walls. The events that led me here replayed in my mind, a relentless montage of my despair, my pain, and my desperation.

I closed my eyes, trying to find a moment of peace, but it eluded me. The path ahead was shrouded in uncertainty, each step forward a venture into the unknown. But amidst the fear and the doubt, there was a flicker of something else – a tiny spark of hope, a distant promise that maybe, just maybe, there was a way out of the darkness.

As I drifted into a restless sleep, the sounds of the facility continued to echo around me, a symphony of shared struggles. And in that chorus of human vulnerability, I realized that I wasn't as alone as I had thought. In this place of healing and pain, I was just one of many, all of us fighting our own battles, all of us searching for a new dawn.

6 UNFAMILIAR TERRITORY

The walls of the state hospital were a stark white, their unyielding surfaces a constant reminder of where I was – a place far removed from anything I had ever known. The air carried a clinical scent, mingled with undertones of despair and disinfectant. Each step I took echoed in the empty corridors, a sound that seemed to resonate with the hollow feeling inside me.

I watched the other patients, each lost in their own world. There was the boy who muttered to himself by the window, his eyes fixed on some unseen vision. A girl paced relentlessly up and down the hallway, her hands wringing a tissue into tatters. Their presence was a mosaic of mental health struggles, a living tapestry that was both daunting and strangely comforting. Here, I wasn't an outlier; I was just another face among many.

I mostly kept to myself, sitting in corners during group activities, my eyes and ears open. The stories I overheard were fragments of lives interrupted, each one a piece of a larger, more complex puzzle. I felt a pull of curiosity, but my own fears held me back, keeping me anchored to my solitude.

That was until I met Michael. He was a year older than me, with a mop of unruly strawberry blonde hair, freckles scattered across his nose and cheeks, and a smirk that seemed permanently etched on his face. He caught me off guard one day in the common area, sliding into the seat next to me.

"New here, huh?" he asked, his tone casual but his eyes sharp, missing nothing.

I nodded, unsure of what to make of him. "Just trying to figure it all out," I admitted, my voice barely above a whisper.

"Good luck with that," Michael chuckled. "I've been here for two weeks, and I'm still as clueless as I was on day one."

There was something about him, a sense of rebellion mixed with an undercurrent of understanding, that drew me in. We started talking, first about inconsequential things – the food, the staff, the rigid schedule of medications and therapy sessions. But soon, our conversations delved deeper, touching on the reasons we were both here.

Michael had a way of making the bleakness of our

situation seem bearable. He joked about the most morose topics, but behind his laughter, I could see the same shadows that haunted me.

We began exploring the facility together, finding little nooks and crannies that offered brief escapes from the watchful eyes of the staff. It was during these explorations that I found myself opening up, sharing pieces of my story with him. It felt like a release, a pressure valve being slowly turned to let out some of the pent-up emotions I'd been carrying.

"So, what brought you here, Sarah?" Michael asked one day as we sat in a hidden corner of the hospital game room. It was a small area with just a couple chairs and books, a tiny oasis in the midst of the sterile environment.

I hesitated, the words catching in my throat. "I... I tried to end it," I said finally, the admission feeling like a weight lifting off my shoulders.

Michael's expression didn't change. He simply nodded, a gesture of understanding that spoke volumes. "Life can be a real bitch, huh?" he said softly. "But I guess we've got a second chance now."

His acceptance was a balm to my soul. In Michael, I had found a kindred spirit, someone who understood the darkness without being consumed by it. Together, we navigated the days, finding solace in each other's company amidst the chaos of our surroundings.

Feeling the weight of the white walls closing in, I glanced at Michael, his eyes reflecting the same restless spark that fueled my own defiance. We shared a silent agreement, a mutual need to break free from the suffocating rules of the hospital. Our rebellion began with stolen moments in the hallways, snatching forbidden items from the snack room. Laughter, our long-lost companion, echoed through the sterile corridors as we indulged in our harmless antics.

But as with all things, the thrill escalated. We swiped a nurse's clipboard, scrawling jokes on the patient charts. Our laughter grew louder, drawing the gaze of the hospital staff like moths to a flame.

The situation spiraled when we found ourselves cornered by the security guards. Michael, with his usual bravado, tried to defuse the tension with a joke, but their stern faces remained unamused. In a swift move, they lunged at him, pinning him to the ground. The sight ignited a fire within me, a protective rage that I couldn't contain.

I lunged forward, my fists flailing in a desperate attempt to free Michael. My actions, however, only served to draw their attention towards me. The guards overpowered me easily, their grips ironclad, as they subdued my rebellion.

The aftermath was a blur. I found myself in a seclusion room, a stark, empty space that mirrored my internal chaos. The walls, devoid of any warmth, stood as a reminder of my impulsive actions. Alone, the adrenaline faded, leaving behind a trail of introspection.

In the silence, my mind wandered to Michael. Our bond had grown in these confined walls, a friendship forged in shared struggles. But now, I questioned the influence we had on each other. Was our rebellious streak a path to freedom, or a descent into chaos?

My thoughts drifted to the events that led me here. Each memory, a piece of the puzzle that was my life, floated in the empty room. My family's worried expressions, the nights spent in restless turmoil, the overwhelming sense of being lost in my own mind. I realized that each decision, each action, had led me to this moment of solitude.

As the hours passed, my anger gave way to exhaustion. My eyelids grew heavy, and the world around me faded. I succumbed to sleep, my dreams a mix of chaotic memories and longing for a sense of understanding.

In that room, confined yet free from external distractions, I began to understand the complexity of my journey. I was more than my rebellious actions, more than the sum of my struggles. As I drifted into sleep, a new awareness dawned within me. My actions, though fueled by a desire for freedom, had consequences. This realization was the first step in a journey towards self-awareness, a path that I knew would be long and tumultuous.

As the night embraced the hospital, my breathing slowed, matching the rhythm of my newfound resolve. In the depths of the seclusion room, I found the beginnings of true introspection, a necessary step in understanding the intricate web of my own psyche.

7 EMBRACING CHANGE

The morning light filtered through the high windows of the therapy room, casting a soft glow on the circle of chairs where we gathered. I sat there, my fingers nervously intertwined, feeling the weight of the moment. Today, I was ready to delve into a memory that had haunted me, a shadow that lingered in the recesses of my mind.

Dr. Ellis, tall and commanding yet approachable, with her long, blonde hair cascading in a mix of curls and waves down to her waist, sat across from me. Her large glasses framed her kind eyes as she offered a patient smile, embodying both professionalism and warmth. 'When you're ready, Sarah,' she said in her soothing tone, nodding encouragingly."

Drawing a deep breath, I closed my eyes, letting the memory surface. "It was the summer before everything changed," I began, my voice barely above a whisper. "The water was calm, reflecting the golden sunset. I was there with... with him." The words caught in my throat, but I pushed through. "That's when it happened, the first time he..."

The room was silent, every ear tuned to my faltering voice. I recounted the details, the pain, the fear, and the betrayal. With each word, the burden lightened, as if I was releasing the memory's hold on me.

Dr. Ellis's words were gentle but empowering. "You've shown incredible strength, Sarah. Acknowledging this pain is a brave step towards healing."

Leaving the therapy room, I felt a sense of liberation. The hallways of the hospital, once a maze of confinement, now felt more like corridors of recovery. I made my way to the art therapy session, where the walls were adorned with expressions of struggle and hope.

I picked up a paintbrush, the bristles soft against my fingers. The canvas before me was blank, a space for my thoughts and feelings. As I painted, the colors told my story - dark hues for my pain and bright ones for my newfound strength. It was a visual journey of my inner world, a representation of the resilience I was building.

In the afternoons, I joined the mindfulness group in the garden. The sun warmed my skin, and the scent of blooming flowers filled the air. We sat in silence, focusing on our breath, learning to be present in the moment. It was during these sessions that I felt a profound peace, a stark contrast to the turmoil that once dominated my mind.

Through these days, my relationship with the hospital staff evolved. Brianna, with her ever-present smile, would often chat with me about books and music. She listened with genuine interest, making me feel seen and heard. And then there was Dr. Ellis, who had become not just my therapist but a trusted confidant. Our sessions were no longer just about treatment but about understanding and growth.

But it was my moments with Michael that brought a different kind of healing. Our conversations delved beyond the walls of the hospital, dreaming of a world outside. We shared our fears and hopes, finding solace in our mutual understanding. Our bond deepened, an unspoken promise of support and care.

The days melted into each other, each one a step further in my journey and a step closer to Michael. Our shared experiences in the hospital had woven a bond between us, a connection that was growing into something more profound, more intimate.

One evening, as twilight painted the sky in shades

of orange and purple, we found ourselves sitting on the small bench in the hospital garden. The air was cool, carrying the scent of jasmine and the distant sound of traffic. Michael was talking about his love for photography, his words painting pictures in the air.

"I used to capture moments," he said, his eyes distant yet bright. "Moments that felt... real. Like they meant something." His voice trailed off, and he turned to me, a soft smile playing on his lips. "But being here, with you, it's like living in those moments."

I felt a warmth spread through my chest. "I never really had moments worth capturing," I replied, my voice barely above a whisper. "But now, I think I'm starting to."

That was the moment our hands found each other, tentative at first, then holding on with a gentle firmness. It was more than a touch; it was an acknowledgment of the comfort and understanding we found in each other.

Our late-night talks became our sanctuary. We shared stories, dreams, and fears under the blanket of stars that peeked through the hospital windows. Michael's humor was a balm to my soul, and my openness seemed to bring him a sense of peace. It was during one of these nights, with the moon casting a soft glow on his face, that he first called me his beacon of hope.

"You know, Sarah," he said, his eyes reflecting the moonlight, "in this place of healing and hurt, you've been my light. You've made this place... bearable."

His words resonated deep within me. "You've been my anchor, Michael. In the chaos of my thoughts, you've been my steadiness."

Our relationship evolved in the shared silence of therapy sessions, in the glances we exchanged when words were too hard to find. We became each other's support system, our presence a constant in the unpredictable world of the hospital.

There were days when the weight of our pasts and the uncertainty of our futures seemed overwhelming. On those days, we would sit side by side, letting our shared strength be our guide. I remember a day when Michael had a breakdown during group therapy. I found him later, sitting alone, his face a canvas of pain and vulnerability.

I sat beside him, not saying a word, just offering my presence. He leaned into me, his head resting on my shoulder, and in that moment, I felt a protectiveness over him, a desire to shield him from his sorrows.

As the days passed, our relationship blossomed into

a quiet love, a love born from shared pain and healing. We didn't need grand gestures or poetic declarations. Our love was in the small things - the shared smiles, the comforting touches, the silent understanding.

The news of my release was bittersweet. The thought of leaving Michael, my anchor in this turbulent sea, filled me with a deep sense of loss. As I packed my few belongings, the reality of our situation settled in. We were about to be separated, each of us stepping into our own uncertain futures.

On my last night, we sat together, our hands intertwined, trying to memorize every detail of the moment.

"Promise me something, Sarah," Michael whispered, his voice thick with emotion. "Promise me you'll remember us, this... whatever this is."

I squeezed his hand, my heart aching. "I promise, Michael. How could I ever forget?"

And in that promise, we found a sliver of hope, a belief that our paths would cross again.

The morning of my release arrived with a tumult of emotions. As I sat on the edge of my neatly made bed, my heart was a battlefield of excitement and fear. The hospital, with its routines and familiar faces, had become a safe haven, a place of healing. Now, stepping out of its doors meant stepping into a world of unknowns.

I stared at the small trash bag that held my belongings, a stark reminder of the transience of my stay here. A knock on the door announced Dr. Ellis's arrival, her presence both comforting and ominous.

"Sarah, it's time for our final session," she said, her voice carrying a note of both pride and solemnity.

We sat across from each other in her office, a space that had witnessed my lowest and highest moments. Dr. Ellis looked at me with a mix of empathy and professionalism.

"You've made remarkable progress, Sarah," she began, her tone gentle. "But the journey ahead requires a different kind of healing, one that the hospital can't provide."

I swallowed hard, my throat tight. "But why can't I go home?" The question had been burning inside me.

"Your home environment... it's complicated. We believe the foster system will provide you with the stability and support you need right now," she explained, her words careful yet firm.

The reasoning made sense, but it did little to ease the ache in my heart. I nodded, fighting back the tears that threatened to spill.

The rest of the morning passed in a blur. I said my goodbyes to the nurses and staff, each farewell a small needle pricking at my heart. Brianna gave me a gentle hug, her usual joviality subdued.

"Take care of yourself, Sarah. You're stronger than you know," she said, her smile tinged with sadness.

And then it was time to say goodbye to Michael. We stood awkwardly in the hallway, the weight of our parting heavy in the air. He took my hand, his grip warm and familiar.

"I don't want to say goodbye," he whispered, his voice cracking.

"Me neither," I replied, my voice barely audible. "But this isn't goodbye, not really. We'll find a way to stay in touch."

We hugged, a long, tight embrace that spoke volumes. I memorized the feel of his arms around me, the scent of his cologne, the warmth of his body. As we parted, I saw the sheen of tears in his eyes.

"I'll miss you, Sarah," he said, his voice thick with emotion.

"I'll miss you more," I replied, trying to smile through my tears.

With a heavy heart, I walked out of the hospital, the building that had been my refuge and my prison. The outside world greeted me with a bright sun and a gentle breeze, a sharp disparity to the storm inside me.

I climbed into the car that would take me to my first foster home, my hands trembling slightly. As we drove away, I watched the hospital shrink in the rearview mirror, a chapter of my life coming to a close.

The road ahead was uncertain, filled with new challenges and fears. But within me, there was a flicker of hope, a belief that I could face whatever lay ahead. With each mile, I left behind the old Sarah, ready to embrace the journey of the new one.

8 THE FOSTER SYSTEM

The first time I stepped into the Daughtry's house, my heart was a fluttering bird in a cage, hopeful yet apprehensive. Mrs. Daughtry, in her sixties with kind wrinkles and mostly gray hair, greeted me with a warm smile that seemed a bit forced, but it was kind nonetheless. Mr. Daughtry, also showing signs of age with gray hair and a gentle demeanor, offered a soft, "Welcome, Sarah," his voice low and steady.

My room was upstairs, a small space with a window overlooking the backyard. The walls were painted a soft blue, and a small desk sat in the corner. It was nothing like my room back home, yet it had a certain charm, a promise of a new beginning.

I unpacked my few belongings, each item a fragment of my past life. As I placed a photo of Michael and me on the desk, a pang of longing hit me. But I shook it off, reminding myself that this was a chance to start anew.

The first few days were a delicate dance of trying to

fit in. I joined the Daughtrys' for dinner, engaging in their light conversation. Mrs. Daughtry was a talker, filling the air with stories about her job as a librarian. Mr. Daughtry was more reserved, offering occasional nods and smiles.

I made an effort to help with household chores, washing dishes, and even attempting to cook a simple meal, which ended in a slightly burnt but edible spaghetti dinner. We all laughed about it, and for a moment, I felt a flicker of belonging.

School was a different battlefield. The halls were a maze of unfamiliar faces and hushed whispers. I felt like a specimen under a microscope, the new girl with a mysterious past. But I kept my head high, attending classes with a quiet determination.

In my English class, I met Jess, a girl with a shy smile and an avid love for books. We bonded over our mutual appreciation for classic literature. She was a gentle soul, and her friendship was a small beacon of light in the overwhelming storm of new experiences.

As the days turned into weeks, I found myself settling into a routine. I would go to school, come back, and spend evenings with the Daughtrys'. They were kind, but there was always an invisible barrier, a line I couldn't cross. A part of me longed to open up to them, to share my story, but another part held back, shackled by the fear of being hurt again.

In my room at night, I would lie awake, staring at the ceiling, my mind racing with thoughts of Michael, the hospital, and the life I had left behind. The darkness was both a blanket and a jail cell, wrapping me in solitude yet trapping me with my own thoughts.

Despite the challenges, there was a glimmer of hope. Maybe, just maybe, I could make this work. Maybe I could find a semblance of normalcy in this new life. But deep down, I knew the road ahead was fraught with shadows and uncertainty, and I couldn't shake off the feeling that my past was always just a step behind, waiting to catch up.

One evening, as the autumn leaves danced outside the window, a simple gesture shattered the fragile semblance of normalcy I had been building. Mr. Daughtry, in an attempt to comfort me during a particularly silent dinner, placed his hand on my shoulder. His touch, though meant to be kind, ignited a firestorm of memories within me.

Panic surged through my veins, my heart racing, and my breath quickening. I jerked away from his touch, my chair scraping loudly against the floor. "Don't touch me," I hissed, my voice laced with fear and anger.

The room fell into a stunned silence. Mr. Daughtry retracted his hand as if he'd been burned, his eyes filled with confusion and hurt. Mrs. Daughtry 's mouth opened, but no words came out. I fled from the room, the echo of my pounding footsteps a stark contrast to the quiet I left behind.

That night, in the solitude of my room, the walls seemed to close in on me. The well-intentioned touch had brought back a flood of unwanted memories, each one a reminder of my vulnerability, of the times I had been powerless.

In the days that followed, I found myself spiraling. My interactions with the Daughtrys' became strained, my responses short and cold. I started coming home late, ignoring their curfew, and their concerned inquiries were met with defiance.

Each act of rebellion was a shield, a way to protect myself from getting too close, from being vulnerable. I was a storm, brewing and uncontainable, driven by a deep-seated fear that had rooted itself in my heart.

The pattern repeated itself as I was removed from the Daughtry's home and shuffled from one foster home to another. Each new family greeted me with smiles and open arms, but the smiles never lasted.

The slightest gesture, a paternal pat on the back or a concerned hand on my arm, would send me into a defensive frenzy.

I became the girl who was too difficult to handle, the one who wouldn't let anyone in. Each goodbye was a mix of relief and regret, a silent acknowledgment that I was running from something I couldn't escape.

In one home, I got into a heated argument with a foster father. His attempt to discipline me for my tardiness turned into a shouting match. "You're not my father, you can't tell me what to do!" I screamed, my voice raw with emotions I couldn't quite understand.

"You're right, I'm not," he said, his voice strained with frustration. "But I am trying to help you, Sarah. Why won't you let us?"

His words struck a chord, but it was buried under layers of fear and mistrust. I left that home the next day, the cycle of distrust and rebellion continuing.

As I moved through the system, a sense of weariness began to take hold. The faces and houses blurred into one another, each new beginning tainted by the inevitability of an end. The optimism I had once clung to was now a distant memory, replaced by a resignation that I was somehow unfixable, destined to be alone.

In the quiet moments of the night, when the world was asleep, and I was left alone with my thoughts, I wondered if I would ever find a place where I belonged, a place where the shadows of my past didn't loom over me, a place where I was wanted. But as each day passed, that hope seemed to fade, like the last rays of sunlight disappearing over the horizon.

In the depths of my ever-shifting world, a sense of despair took root. The foster homes, each a temporary shelter, became mere backdrops to my inner turmoil. With every new placement, a veil of numbness thickened around me, and in a desperate bid to feel something, anything, I turned back to the one thing I thought I had left behind – self-harm.

It started small, a scratch here, a cut there, hidden beneath long sleeves and fabricated smiles. The pain was a release, a momentary escape from the chaos that churned inside me. Each line on my skin was a tangible representation of the turmoil I couldn't express in words.

But the relief was fleeting, and soon, I found myself seeking control in other aspects of my life. Food became the enemy, an entity I could defy. I started skipping meals, my excuses ready for the concerned questions from my latest foster parents. "I'm not hungry," I would say, or "I already ate at school." The lies slipped out easily, but each one was a brick in the wall I was building around myself.

At school, my clothes hung loose on my frame, and dark circles took residence under my eyes. My teachers' furrowed brows and whispered conversations didn't escape my notice. Mrs. Adler, my English teacher, approached me one day after class, her eyes filled with a mix of worry and kindness.

"Sarah, is everything alright? You seem... different lately," she asked, her voice soft yet insistent.

"I'm fine," I replied, my voice a flat monotone, belying the storm inside me. I avoided her gaze, focusing on the worn edges of my textbook.

But Mrs. Adler persisted, "You know you can talk to me, right? If something's bothering you..."

I cut her off, "Really, I'm fine. Thanks." I gathered my things quickly, escaping her concern and the truth I wasn't ready to face.

The nights were the hardest. Alone in my room, the silence was deafening, and my thoughts were loud and unrelenting. I found myself longing for the hospital, for Michael, for a time when things seemed simpler. But those days were gone, replaced by a reality I couldn't escape.

One night, the dam broke. The pent-up emotions, the fear, the loneliness, all spilled out in a torrent of pain. I harmed myself more severely than I had intended, the shock of it momentarily pulling me out of my fog. I stared at the injury, a sense of horror mixing with the all-too-familiar relief.

That was the moment my current foster parents found me, their faces etched with shock and fear. I remember the flurry of activity, the rush to the emergency room, the blinding lights, and the hushed voices.

As I lay in the hospital bed, a sense of déjà vu enveloping me, the reality of my situation sank in. My journey had come full circle, bringing me back to the starting point. The sense of defeat was overwhelming, but beneath it, there was a flicker of something else - a desperate hope for salvation, for a chance to heal what I had broken.

The morning after my emergency room visit, I sat in the living room of the foster home, a blanket wrapped around my shoulders. The room was quiet, except for the ticking of the clock and the occasional passing car outside. Mr. and Mrs. Larson, my current foster parents, sat across from me, their faces etched with concern. Beside them was Ms. Henderson, the social worker who had been a constant in my turbulent journey through the foster system.

"Sarah, we're all here because we care about you, and we're worried about your safety," Ms. Henderson began, her voice steady yet filled with empathy. "What happened last night was serious. We need to make sure you're in a place where you can get the help you need."

I looked down at my hands, folded in my lap, my fingers tracing the fabric of the blanket. I knew they were right, but admitting it felt like acknowledging a failure I wasn't ready to face.

Mr. Larson spoke next, his voice gentle. "We want to help you, Sarah, but we're not equipped to provide the care you need right now."

Mrs. Larson added, her eyes moist, "You're not alone in this, dear. We just want what's best for you."

The room felt heavy with their words, each one a reminder of the chaos I had brought into their lives. I swallowed the lump in my throat and nodded, unable to find the words to express the turmoil inside me.

The decision was made. I was to return to the state hospital, a place I had associated with both healing and confinement. The drive there was a blur, the world outside passing by in a haze of colors and shapes.

As the car pulled up to the hospital, a sense of familiarity enveloped me. The building stood tall and imposing, yet it was a refuge in its own right. I stepped out, the doors opening to welcome me back.

The lobby was much the same as I remembered, the walls holding echoes of my past stay. Sophia, a staff member, who had been a comforting presence during my previous time here, greeted me with a sad smile.

"Welcome back, Sarah. We've missed you," she said, her voice tinged with concern.

I managed a weak smile, "Thanks, Sophia. It's good to see you."

As we walked through the corridors, the sounds and sights of the hospital wrapped around me like an old blanket - familiar, yet not entirely comforting. We passed patients and staff, each absorbed in their own worlds, yet part of the tapestry that was this place of healing and pain.

My room was a small, private space, with a window

overlooking the hospital grounds. The bed was neatly made, the sheets crisp and clean. I sat down, the mattress yielding softly under my weight.

Sophia assured me, "We'll take good care of you, Sarah. You're in a safe place now."

Her words were meant to comfort me, but they also underscored the reality of my situation. I was back where I started, yet everything had changed. The girl who had left this hospital with a glimmer of hope was now a shell of her former self, broken by the world she had so desperately wanted to be a part of.

As Sophia left, closing the door softly behind her, I lay back on the bed, staring at the ceiling. The hospital, once a place of healing, now felt like a reminder of my failures. But beneath the layers of defeat and despair, there was a flicker of something else - a faint hope that maybe, possibly, this was where I needed to be to find my way back to myself.

9 RELAPSE AND REUNION

The familiar halls of the hospital felt different this time, as if they resonated with my sense of defeat. My steps were heavy, each one echoing my reluctance to be back in this place that signified both a haven and a prison. The stark white walls, once a symbol of hope and recovery, now seemed to mock my relapse.

My room was a small, clinical space, devoid of personality. I sat on the edge of the bed, staring out the window at the grey sky, feeling a profound sense of isolation. This wasn't just a physical return to the hospital; it was an admission of my failure to cope with the world outside.

The staff, familiar yet distant, introduced a new regimen to address my disordered eating. Nurse Reynolds, with her kind eyes and gentle manner, sat down beside me with a food chart. "Sarah, we need to ensure you're getting the nutrition you need," she explained, her tone empathetic yet firm.

I looked at the chart, a structured plan of meals and snacks, and felt a surge of resistance. "I don't need this," I muttered, the words a weak defense against my own vulnerability.

"We're here to help you, not control you," Nurse Reynolds replied, sensing my discomfort. "But we also need to make sure you're healthy."

The counseling sessions were a stark contrast to my previous engagements. Dr. Ellis' office, once a place where I had opened up about my deepest fears and hopes, now felt like an interrogation room. I sat there, arms crossed, my responses monosyllabic.

"Sarah, I know this is hard for you, but shutting down won't help," Dr. Ellis said, her voice a blend of concern and professional detachment. "We want to understand what you're going through so we can support you."

I just shrugged, the words stuck in my throat, a tangled mess of emotions I couldn't unravel.

As the days passed, the routine of the hospital enveloped me, but the sense of progress I once felt was replaced by a numb resignation. The group therapy sessions, the art classes, even the moments of solitude in the garden, all felt like motions I was going through without any real connection.

Then, one day, as I was wandering the halls, lost in my own thoughts, I turned a corner and there he was – Michael. His face lit up in surprise, a mix of happiness and concern etching his features.

"Sarah? You're back!" he screamed, stepping towards me.

His voice, a familiar melody, broke through my walls for a moment. "Yeah, I'm back," I replied, my voice a whisper.

We sat in the common area, an awkward silence growing between us. I could feel his eyes on me, filled with questions he didn't dare ask.

"I missed you," he finally said, his voice low.

I looked up, meeting his gaze. "I missed you too," I admitted, the truth of the words surprising even myself.

But the ease we once shared seemed lost, buried under the weight of my recent experiences. I was a different person now, more broken, more guarded. And as much as I wanted to lean on him, to find solace in his presence, I couldn't shake off the feeling of being utterly alone in my struggle.

The days merged into one another, a blur of therapy, meals, and long periods of introspection. I was back in the place that had once given me hope, but now I felt like I was at the bottom of a deep well, trying to climb up but slipping back down with every attempt.

The days following our reunion were a complex dance of reconnection and distance. Michael and I found ourselves together often, sometimes in comfortable silence, other times attempting to bridge the gap that our absence and experiences had created between us.

One evening, we sat in the dimly lit common room, the flickering light from the television casting shadows on the walls. Michael was talking about his own journey since I left, his words tinged with a vulnerability he hadn't shown before.

"It's been tough, Sarah," he admitted, his eyes not meeting mine. "When you left, it felt like I lost a part of myself."

I listened, my heart aching with a mix of guilt and affection. "I never wanted to leave you," I said quietly, the truth of the words echoing in the hollow space inside me.

He turned to look at me, his gaze intense. "But you're different now, Sarah. Like you're here, but not really."

His observation stung because it was true. Since

coming back, I had been a shell of my former self, guarded and introspective, afraid to let anyone, even Michael, see the turmoil inside me.

"I don't know how to be the old Sarah anymore, Michael," I confessed, my voice barely above a whisper. "Too much has happened."

He reached out, his hand hesitating in the air before gently resting on mine. "I don't need the old Sarah. I just need you, whoever you are now."

His words were a balm to my bruised soul, but they also filled me with an unease. How could I lean on him when I was so broken myself?

As we spent more time together, the dynamics of our relationship continued to evolve. Michael was more protective, always watching me with a concern that was both comforting and suffocating. I found myself pulling away at times, needing space to breathe, to figure out who I was in this maze of healing and pain.

Despite the tension, there were moments of genuine connection, brief glimpses of the ease we once shared. We would laugh at a joke, share stories from our past, or sit in silence, simply enjoying each other's presence. But these moments were fleeting, overshadowed by the unspoken fears and uncertainties that lay between us.

One afternoon, we sat in the garden, the autumn sun casting a warm glow over the fading flowers. I watched a butterfly flit from blossom to blossom, its delicate wings a stark contrast to the chaos of my thoughts.

"Sarah," Michael began, his voice hesitant, "do you ever think about the future? About what happens when we leave this place?"

I turned to look at him, his face earnest and hopeful. "I try not to," I admitted. "The future feels like this vast, unknown ocean, and I'm just... floating, not knowing where I'm headed."

He nodded, understanding in his eyes. "I get scared too. But I like to think that maybe, things will change, and we could face that ocean together."

His words were a promise, an anchor in the uncertainty that was my life. But they were also a reminder of how much I had changed, how unsure I was of my ability to be part of anyone's future, even Michael's.

Our relationship had become a complex tapestry of care, concern, and unspoken fears. We were two people who had found each other in the midst of our struggles, yet now stood at the crossroads, uncertain of the path ahead.

As the days at the hospital unfolded in a monotonous rhythm, marked by therapy sessions and silent meals, an underlying current of anxiety began to build within me. It was a premonition that something was about to disrupt the fragile equilibrium I had been clinging to.

This apprehension materialized one quiet afternoon when Nurse Reynolds called me to the nurse's station and pointed to the payphone hanging on the wall. "It's your mother." My heart sank. I hadn't spoken to her since returning to the hospital, and the suddenness of the call filled me with a sense of dread. Taking a deep breath, I braced myself for the conversation, unaware of how deeply it would shake the foundations of my already tenuous state of mind.

The phone in my hand felt like a lead weight as I heard the familiar yet distant voice of my mother on the other end. "Sarah, we need to talk," she said, her voice strained with a mixture of concern and disappointment.

I braced myself, the walls of the room seeming to close in around me. "Hi, Mom," I replied, my voice a mere whisper, betraying the turmoil churning inside me.

There was a pause, heavy with unspoken words before she continued. "I heard about what happened, about you going back to the hospital. We're all very disappointed, Sarah. We thought you were getting better."

Her words stung, each one a piercing reminder of my failures. "I'm trying, Mom," I said, the fight in my voice diminished to a plea. "It's just been really hard."

"Hard?" Her voice rose slightly, tinged with frustration. "Do you have any idea how hard it's been for us? We're trying to be a family again, but you keep running away from your problems."

The accusation hung in the air, a tangible force that squeezed my heart. "I'm not running away," I countered, my voice breaking. "I'm struggling, Mom. Can't you see that?"

There was a sigh on the other end, one that spoke of tired battles and worn patience. "We all have our struggles, Sarah. But at some point, you need to start taking responsibility for your actions."

The conversation spiraled, each word from her a confirmation of my deepest fears - that I was a disappointment, a burden. I fought back tears, trying to defend myself, to explain the pain and confusion that ruled my life. But it was like speaking to a wall, my words failing to bridge the gap between us.

The call ended with a hollow "Take care of yourself, Sarah," leaving me in a void of isolation and despair. I hung up the phone, feeling more alone than ever, and ran down the hall. The walls of my room no longer felt like a sanctuary; they were a prison, echoing with the words of a conversation that had shattered the fragile hope I had been clinging to.

In the days that followed, I retreated further into myself. The progress I had made in therapy unraveled, my sessions reduced to silent sittings with a counselor who tried in vain to reach me. I avoided Michael, unable to bear the weight of his concern and the guilt that came with it.

My thoughts spiraled, a relentless storm of self-doubt and worthlessness. The hospital, once a place of healing, now felt like a monument to my failures. I wandered its halls like a ghost, disconnected from the world around me.

A staff member, Tammy, noticed the change in me. "Sarah, you're not alone in this," she said one day, her voice laced with worry. "You have people here who care about you, who want to help you."

But her words felt distant, like a lifeline thrown from a faraway shore. I was drowning in an ocean of my own making, and I didn't know how to swim back to the surface.

As I lay in my bed each night, staring at the ceiling, I wondered if there was a way out of this maze of despair. The phone call with my mother had been a mirror, reflecting a reality I didn't want to face - that perhaps I was truly beyond redemption, beyond the reach of love and understanding.

The chapter of my life that had started with hope and the promise of healing was turning into a narrative of pain and alienation, a story I didn't know how to rewrite.

In the days following the call, I found myself wandering the labyrinth of my own thoughts, each turn leading me deeper into a maze of self-doubt and despair. The words from my mother echoed in my mind, a relentless reminder of my perceived failures. I felt like an outsider in my own family, a lost piece that no longer fit into the puzzle.

During my therapy sessions, my usual reticence was replaced by a hollow silence. Dr. Ellis, ever patient, watched me with a concern that seemed to fill the room. "Sarah, I can see you're struggling," she said gently during one session. "Want to talk about what's going on?"

I shook my head, my gaze fixed on a point somewhere beyond the walls of the room. "It's pointless," I muttered.

"It's not pointless," she countered softly. "Talking about it, understanding it, that's how we start to heal."

Her words, meant to be encouraging, felt like a weight. I sighed, the sound heavy with weariness. "My family... they don't want me. I'm just a burden to them."

Dr. Ellis leaned forward, her expression earnest. "Families can be complicated, Sarah. Sometimes, they might not know how to express their concerns or fears. It doesn't mean they don't care."

"But it feels like they've given up on me," I whispered, the admission a crack in the dam holding back my emotions.

"Maybe they're just trying to find their way, just like you are," she suggested. "Healing isn't just your journey. It affects those around you too."

Her words planted a seed of thought in my mind. Perhaps my family's reactions were rooted in their own struggles, their own inability to navigate the turbulent waters of mental illness.

In the following days, Michael's presence became a constant in the shifting sands of my life. He tried to reach out, to offer comfort, but I was trapped in a shell of my own making.

One evening, as we sat in the fading light of the common room, he reached for my hand. "Sarah, I'm here for you. You know that, right?"

I pulled away, a reflex born of an instinct to protect myself from more pain. "I can't, Michael," I said, my voice a whisper of despair. "I can't drag you into this mess."

"It's not about being dragged in," he said, his voice laced with frustration and care. "It's about being there for each other, no matter what."

His words, so full of sincerity, should have been a comfort, but they only served to remind me of how far I had fallen, how lost I felt.

As the chapter of my life at the hospital continued, I found myself at a crossroads. The path behind me was littered with the debris of my past actions and choices, while the road ahead was shrouded in uncertainty.

But amidst the turmoil, a glimmer of understanding began to emerge. Dr. Ellis' words about family, Michael's unwavering support, they were beacons in the darkness, guiding me toward a deeper understanding of myself and the complex web of relationships that defined my life.

Perhaps healing wasn't just about mending the broken pieces within me. Maybe it was also about learning to navigate the intricate dance of human connections, about understanding that everyone was fighting their own battles, just as I was fighting mine.

In the quiet moments of reflection, I started to see that my journey was far from over. It was a path fraught with challenges, but also lined with opportunities for growth and understanding. And maybe, if I allowed myself to heal, this could be the first step towards finding my way back to a life filled with hope and meaning.

10 A BROKEN BOND

The days ahead didn't feel as hopeful and the echoes of my mother's disheartening words still lingered in my mind, the weight of my own emotions became a suffocating shroud. Each step through the hospital's sterile corridors felt heavier, each thought more oppressive. The stark white walls, once a symbol of recovery, now seemed to mock my stagnation. I was caught in a whirlpool of self-doubt and fear, with each interaction with Michael adding to the swirling chaos.

Our conversations, once filled with ease and understanding, had turned into a series of cautious exchanges. We were like two actors on a stage, reciting our lines with a semblance of normalcy, but beneath the surface, there was a tumult of unspoken anxieties and suppressed frustrations.

One evening, as we sat in the game room's dim light, the tension reached a breaking point. We were discussing something trivial, a mere facade for the storm brewing within. Michael's attempts to lighten the mood felt like nails on the chalkboard of my frayed nerves.

"Why do you keep doing this?" I suddenly burst out, my voice a sharp crack in the quiet room. "Pretending like everything is okay when it's not!"

Michael looked at me, taken aback by my outburst. His eyes, usually a wellspring of empathy, now reflected a mix of confusion and hurt. "Sarah, I'm just trying to help," he replied, his voice a mixture of concern and bewilderment.

But his words, meant to be soothing, only fanned the flames of my agitation. I felt cornered, trapped by the expectations I perceived in his words, and overwhelmed by the facade I felt forced to maintain. "You can't help me, Michael! Nobody can," I snapped, my voice rising in a crescendo of desperation and fear. "I don't love you. I never did."

The words hung in the air, a toxic cloud that enveloped us both. Michael's face crumpled, the pain in his expression cutting me deeper than I cared to admit. But I was too engulfed in my own turmoil to offer any solace or retract my words.

He stood up abruptly, his chair scraping against the floor with a jarring sound. For a moment, he just stared at me, the hurt in his eyes a mirror to my own inner turmoil. Then, without a word, he turned and walked away, his withdrawal a silent testament to the fracture that had just occurred between us.

The sight of Michael's retreating back, his shoulders hunched in a way that spoke volumes of his hurt, sent a ripple of fear through me. The room, still echoing with the remnants of our heated exchange, felt suffocating. I remained seated, paralyzed by a tumult of emotions. My outburst, intended as a shield, now felt like a weapon I had turned against both of us.

As the door closed behind him with a soft click, a stark realization dawned on me. Michael, with his own battles and vulnerabilities, might not just retreat into the solitude of his room; he might retreat into the depths of his despair. The thought struck me like a physical blow, leaving me breathless with fear.

My mind raced, conjuring up scenarios each more frightening than the last. Michael had always been the stronger one, the one who could pull us both through the darkness. But what if my words had pushed him over an edge? The possibility that he might harm himself, acting on a moment of impulsive despair, was a thought I couldn't bear.

I stood up abruptly, the chair scraping against the floor in my haste. My heart pounded in my chest, each beat a drum of panic. I had to find him, to make sure he was okay, to apologize for the words that now tasted like poison on my tongue.

The hallways of the hospital were a blur as I hurried towards Michael's room. My steps were quick, driven by an urgency that left no room for doubt or hesitation. The fluorescent lights overhead cast stark shadows on the walls, mirroring the darkness that seemed to encroach upon my heart.

Reaching his hallway, I was stopped by a staff member named Lucy, I hesitated for a brief moment, my voice trembling as I began to tell her what I said and why I needed to go check on him and apologize.

"Sarah, you know you can't go down the boy's hall, but don't worry. I will go check on him now and bring him back so the two of you can talk."

My heart sank, fear tightening its grip. What if he didn't want to see me? What if my words had severed the last thread of our connection?

I sat waiting for Lucy to come and tell me Michael was okay but several minutes had passed and still, no response came. The silence was a heavy weight, pressing down on me with all the force of my regrets and fears. In that moment, sitting by myself, the magnitude of what I had done – what I might have caused – was overwhelming.

Fighting back tears, I leaned against the table in front of me, the cool surface a small comfort against the storm of emotions raging inside me. I closed my eyes, whispering a silent plea into the void. "Please be okay, Michael. Please."

The minutes stretched on, each one an eternity of waiting and fear. The possibility that I might have pushed Michael to a point of no return was a reality I wasn't prepared to face. But as I sat there, alone in the dimly lit game room, I knew that this was the consequence of my actions, the price of allowing fear and pain to dictate my words.

And so, I waited, my heart a symphony of hope and dread, praying for a sign that Michael was still there, that we still had a chance to mend the fractured bond between us.

The game room, with its muted colors and scattered board games, felt like a bubble of stillness amidst the chaos that was about to erupt. I sat there, my thoughts a whirlpool of fear and regret, fixated on Michael's hall. Each second that passed was a sharp prick of anxiety, wondering what lay beyond that barrier.

Suddenly, the tranquility shattered. The hallways erupted into a frenzy of activity, the calmness violently swept away by a tide of urgency. The sharp, piercing sound of the intercom cut through the air, a cold, impersonal voice announcing, "Code blue, Room 17."

My heart seized. Room 17 – Michael's room. The words were a cruel echo of my worst fears. Time seemed to slow, each second stretching into an agonizing eternity. I stood up, my body moving on its own accord, driven by a visceral need to know, to see.

As I stepped into the hallway, the scene before me was one of controlled pandemonium. Nurses and doctors rushed past, their faces set in grim lines of determination. The urgency in their steps, the gravity of their expressions – it was a dance of life and death, and I was an unwilling spectator.

My feet carried me towards Room 17, each step fueled by a growing dread. The possibility that Michael might have done something drastic in the wake of our argument, that my words could have been the catalyst, was a thought too devastating to bear.

I neared the room, my breath catching in my throat. The door was ajar, and through the sliver of space, I could see the flurry of medical staff, the flash of blue scrubs and the glint of medical equipment. Voices overlapped in a cacophony of urgency, but it was the underlying current of desperation that chilled me to the bone.

"Stay with us, Michael," someone said, the words a stark contrast to the clinical beep of monitors.

Michael. The name was a dagger to my heart. The realization that I might be witnessing the worst possible consequence of our fractured bond was a terror that gripped me with icy fingers. My mind reeled, unable to fully grasp the gravity of the situation.

I stood there, frozen, as the echoes of the commotion inside the room washed over me. The weight of the moment, the fear that my actions might have led to this, was a burden too heavy to bear. Guilt, fear, and shock intertwined, forming a noose of dread around my neck.

In the midst of the chaos, a nurse noticed me, her eyes softening for a moment in recognition of my distress. "You need to wait outside," she said gently, yet firmly, guiding me back down the hall.

I complied numbly, moving away from the room as if in a trance. The hallway, once a simple corridor in a hospital, now felt like a liminal space between hope and despair.

The chapter of my life that I had hoped would lead to healing and reconciliation was turning into a nightmarish spiral. The consequences of my words, my actions, were crashing down around me, leaving me in a state of shock and dread.

As I stood there, the cold floor beneath my feet and the distant sounds of the code blue echoing in my ears, I was engulfed by a sense of helplessness. The realization that I might have lost Michael forever, not to a parting of ways, but to something much more final, was a thought too harrowing to face.

In that moment, the hospital transformed. It was no longer a place of healing; it was a witness to the tragedy of human frailty, of words spoken in fear, and bonds broken in pain. And I, a solitary figure amidst the chaos, was left to grapple with the reality of a world that had irrevocably changed.

11 A GRIEF-STRICKEN DECENT

The moment the words left Lucy's lips - "Michael... he's gone, Sarah" - my world came to a standstill. Those words echoed in my head, bouncing around in a hollow space that seemed to expand with each repetition. "Gone." The finality of it was unfathomable, a concept too vast and dark for my mind to grasp.

I stood there, in the dimly lit hallway, feeling a surreal detachment from my body. My hands were trembling, my vision blurred as if I were underwater. The bustling sounds of the hospital, the distant yells and arguments, the muffled footsteps of staff - all of it faded into a background hum, insignificant against the deafening silence that Michael's absence had created.

"No, that can't be right," I heard my own voice say, distant and unfamiliar. It was a reflex, a desperate clutch at any thread of hope. But Lucy's face, etched with genuine sorrow and sympathy, told me that my plea for it to be a mistake was in vain.

The walk back to my room was a blur. My legs moved mechanically, carrying me through a space that suddenly felt alien and oppressive. The walls seemed to close in on me, the air thick and heavy with an unspeakable loss.

Once inside my room, the numbness began to give way to a torrent of emotions. Disbelief, confusion, and an overwhelming sense of guilt crashed over me. The last time I saw Michael, the last words we shared - they replayed in my mind, a torturous loop of what-ifs and if-onlys.

"How could this happen?" I whispered to the empty room, my voice breaking. The four walls bore silent witness to my unraveling, the only companions in my descent into despair.

I sat on the edge of the bed, my hands clasped tightly in my lap, as if holding them together could keep me from falling apart. Tears streamed down my face, unchecked and unheeded. Each one was a testament to the depth of the bond we had shared and the void that Michael's departure had left.

In those moments, time lost all meaning. The world outside continued its relentless march, indifferent to the ground that had shifted beneath me. The loss of Michael was a chasm that seemed to grow deeper with each passing second, an abyss that threatened to swallow me whole.

As the initial shock slowly ebbed, a heavy blanket of grief settled on my shoulders. It was a weight I had never known, an unbearable heaviness that made even the simplest act of breathing feel like a monumental task.

That night, as I lay in my bed staring at the ceiling, the silence was oppressive. It was broken only by the sound of my own sobs, each one a raw, jagged sound that seemed to tear from the very depths of my soul.

The reality of a world without Michael was a landscape bleak and desolate, a terrain I was ill-equipped to navigate. The future, once a horizon of possibilities, now loomed before me as an endless night, starless and void of hope.

In that room, in the depths of despair and shock, I began to understand the true nature of loss. It was not just the absence of a person; it was the absence of every dream, every moment, every possibility that could have been. And as I succumbed to a fitful, restless sleep, I realized that this was just the beginning of a journey through grief, a path I would have to walk, one painful step at a time.

The days following Michael's passing merged into a

colorless blur, each indistinguishable from the next. Grief hung over me like a shroud, a constant companion in my every waking moment. It infiltrated my dreams, turning them into nightmarish echoes of reality where I relived our last conversation, each word a sharpened dagger to my heart.

My emotions were a tumultuous sea, waves of guilt, anger, and sorrow crashing over me with relentless ferocity. In quiet moments, guilt gnawed at me, a persistent whisper that perhaps I could have done something, said something, to change the tragic course of events. Anger flared too, irrational and fiery, directed at the world, at Michael, at myself. But beneath it all lay an unending sadness, a profound sense of loss that hollowed out my soul.

Physically, I was a shadow of myself. Meals went untouched, the very thought of food turning my stomach. Sleep became elusive, a sought-after escape that, when it did come, brought little relief. I would wake from restless slumber feeling just as tired, if not more. My body felt heavy, each movement an effort, as if I were wading through molasses.

I withdrew from the world around me. The hospital activities, once a small respite from my inner turmoil, now held no appeal. I skipped group therapy sessions, stayed silent during one-on-ones with my counselor, and spent hours lying on my bed, staring blankly at the ceiling. The world outside my window continued its rhythm, but I was no longer a part of it. I was in a limbo of grief, disconnected from everything and everyone.

Even the well-intentioned attempts of the hospital staff to engage me were met with apathy. Nurse Reynolds would come into my room with a gentle, "How are we doing today, Sarah?" But her words, kind as they were, felt distant, unable to penetrate the thick fog of my grief.

"I'm fine," I would respond mechanically, my voice devoid of emotion. It was a lie, a mask I wore to keep the world at bay.

I could feel the concern of the staff, the unspoken worries that hovered in the air whenever they were near. But their presence, their efforts to reach me, were like rays of sunlight trying to pierce through a dense canopy of clouds. I was lost in my own darkness, unreachable, untouchable.

In those endless days and nights, grief became my identity. It defined me, shaped my existence. I was no longer just Sarah; I was a vessel of sorrow, adrift in a sea of despair. The vibrant colors of life had faded to monochrome, and joy, once a familiar friend, was now a stranger.

And so, I existed in a state of suspended animation, caught between the life I once knew and the unbearable reality of the present. The world moved on around me, but I remained static, a prisoner of my own anguish, waiting for the day when the weight of my grief might lessen, even if just a little.

In the weeks that followed, my world shrank to the confines of the hospital, to the four walls of my room, and to the turbulent landscape of my mind. The people around me - my family, the friends I had made here, the staff - became distant figures, moving in a world I no longer felt part of. I pushed them away, each interaction a reminder of the gaping hole Michael had left behind.

When my family visited, their words of comfort and attempts at conversation felt like they were spoken in a foreign language. I saw their pain, their effort to reach me, but it was as if I were at the bottom of a deep ocean, their voices muffled and distorted by the water above.

"How are you holding up, Sarah?" my mother would ask, her eyes brimming with concern.

"I'm fine," would be my automatic response, a protective reflex to keep her from seeing the depth of my despair.

But I wasn't fine. Far from it. The loneliness was a constant ache, a reminder that Michael, the one person who had truly understood me, was gone. In my isolation, I found a cold comfort, a place where I could nurse my grief without the need to pretend or put on a brave face.

My refuge, my escape, became the memories of Michael. I surrounded myself with them, creating a shrine in my mind where I could retreat. I would spend hours poring over old photos of us, tracing the contours of his face with my finger as if I could bring him back to life through sheer will.

There was a box under my bed, filled with mementos - a crumpled note he had passed me in class, a small rock he had picked up on one of our walks. Each item was a tangible piece of a past that was no longer accessible, a past that had been stolen from me.

In those moments, surrounded by these remnants of our shared past, I found a bittersweet solace. They were painful reminders of what I had lost, yet they were also the only connection I had left to Michael. Clinging to them was like holding onto the pieces of a shattered dream, trying to piece it back together even though I knew it was impossible.

But even in these escapes, reality would eventually intrude. The pain would seep back in, a tide that no amount of memories could hold back. And with each return to the present, the void left by Michael's absence seemed to grow larger, more consuming.

I was caught in a cycle of grief and reminiscence, each day a repetition of the last. My life had become a monochrome existence, punctuated only by the vivid flashes of memory that served as both a refuge and a prison.

In this chapter of my life, I was learning the hardest lesson of all - that some losses are irrevocable, and that the shadow they cast can touch every corner of your world. It was a lesson written in tears and whispered in the silence of a room filled with ghosts of a past that would never return.

Each day in the hospital blurred into the next, a continuous loop of despair and detachment. My mental state, already fragile, began to crumble under the weight of unrelenting grief. The world outside my window carried on in its relentless rhythm, but inside, time seemed to stand still, each tick of the clock a reminder of the emptiness that engulfed me.

Depression clung to me like a second skin, a constant companion that whispered words of hopelessness and despair. Waking each morning was like emerging into a world devoid of color, where the promise of a new day held no meaning. I existed in a limbo, caught between the pain of the present and the memories of the past.

Self-care became an inconsequential thought, lost in the tumult of my inner world. My hair hung in unkempt tangles, and my clothes bore the stains of days gone by. The mirror reflected a stranger, a hollow-eyed ghost of the person I once was.

The staff at the hospital, their faces etched with concern and frustration, tried to coax me into taking care of myself. "Sarah, you need to shower," Nurse Reynolds would urge gently. But her words seemed to come from a distant place, muffled and insignificant against the roar of my inner turmoil.

Then came the day when their patience reached its limit. I remember sitting on my bed, lost in a fog of apathy, when the door opened abruptly. Two security guards stood there, their expressions stern. "It's time for a shower, Sarah," one of them said, his voice brooking no argument.

Panic surged through me, a primal fear awakened by their imposing presence. "No, please," I whispered, my voice trembling. "I don't want to."

But my pleas fell on deaf ears. They advanced, their hands reaching out to guide me forcefully. The touch of their hands on my skin triggered a flood of memories, each one a reminder of a past filled with helplessness and fear.

I screamed a raw, visceral sound that echoed off the walls. "Don't touch me!" The words were a desperate cry, a defense against a perceived threat that loomed large in my traumatized mind.

Hearing the commotion, Lucy rushed in, her eyes widening in alarm at the scene before her. "Stop! Let her go," she commanded, her voice a sharp contrast to her usual calm demeanor.

The guards hesitated, looking between me and the staff member. "She needs to clean up," one of them protested, but Lucy was firm.

"She's been through enough. Leave us," she said, her tone leaving no room for argument.

The guards left reluctantly, and Lucy turned to me, her expression softening. "Sarah, it's okay. You're safe," she soothed, her presence a calming force in the chaos.

Sobbing, I clung to her, my body racked with tremors of fear and relief. She held me gently, her touch a stark contrast to the harshness of the guards. "I'm sorry, Sarah. I didn't know they would... I'm here now."

In that moment, cradled in the safety of her embrace, the fear ebbed slightly, replaced by a weary exhaustion. Lucy understood, she knew of the shadows that haunted me, the scars left by a past that still held power over me.

As she helped me to the bathroom, her kindness a guiding light in the darkness of my fear, I realized how far I had fallen, how lost I was in the labyrinth of my own grief and trauma. The path back to myself seemed an impossible journey, but in the gentle care of Lucy, there was a flicker of hope, a reminder that even in the depths of despair, compassion could still find a way through.

In the solitude of my room, with the world outside continuing its indifferent march, I found myself wrestling with questions too heavy for my young mind. The concept of life and death, once distant and abstract, now loomed over me, a relentless shadow. Why did Michael have to go? Why did life seem so arbitrarily cruel? The questions circled in my head like vultures over a barren landscape, picking at the remnants of my shattered beliefs.

Nights were the worst. In the quiet darkness, thoughts that lay dormant in the daylight hours emerged, each one a piercing needle of doubt and confusion. I would stare at the ceiling, my mind a battleground of existential queries. The unfairness of it all weighed heavily on me, a burden that seemed to grow with each passing moment.

In those endless hours of introspection, I grappled with the fragility of human existence. Michael's absence was a stark reminder of how fleeting life could be, how suddenly it could all be taken away. The realization filled me with a deep-seated fear, a dread of the unknown that lurked around every corner.

Yet, amid this turmoil, there was a part of me, small and flickering, that yearned to move beyond the grief. I wanted to find a way to honor Michael's memory, to make sense of the senseless. But the path forward was obscured by the dense fog of my sorrow.

"I don't know how to do this without him," I confessed to Dr. Ellis during one of our sessions. My voice was a mere whisper, laden with despair.

She looked at me, her eyes kind but unflinching. "Sarah, finding meaning after such a loss isn't easy. It's a journey, one that's uniquely yours. But remember, you're not alone in it."

Her words were meant to be comforting, but they felt like a reminder of the daunting task ahead. How could I find meaning in a world that had taken Michael from me? How could I look to the future when the present was so engulfed in pain?

It was a conflict that raged within me, a war

between the desire to heal and the inability to envision a life without the person who had been my anchor. Each day was a struggle against the tide of my own emotions, a fight to keep my head above the waters of despair.

In my quieter moments, I would sit by the window, watching the world outside. The people I saw seemed to move with purpose, their lives untainted by the tragedy that had befallen me. I envied them, even as I felt disconnected from them, a spectator in a play where everyone else knew their lines.

The struggle to find meaning in the aftermath of Michael's death was a journey through uncharted territory. It was a path fraught with pain and uncertainty, but it was also a road that I knew I had to travel. With each small step, each moment of reflection, I was slowly piecing together a new understanding of the world and my place in it.

But the journey was far from over. The road ahead was long and uncertain, a path that I would walk with trepidation and hope. In the depths of my despair, I was beginning to understand that finding meaning in loss was not just about answering the questions that haunted me. It was about learning to live with them, to accept the uncertainty and to find strength in the struggle.

As I gazed out the window, the first rays of dawn breaking through the darkness, I realized that this was just the beginning. The journey to find meaning, to rebuild myself in the wake of tragedy, was a journey that I would walk one day at a time, with each step a testament to my resilience and my willingness to face the unknown.

12 TENTATIVE STEPS FORWARD

The morning light filtered softly through the blinds of Dr. Ellis' office, casting a serene glow over the room. I sat there, my hands clasped in my lap, feeling a strange mixture of apprehension and resolve. This was a different Sarah who entered the therapy room - one who was tired of being ensnared in the relentless grip of grief.

Dr. Ellis, with her calm demeanor and patient eyes, gave me a small, encouraging smile. "Good morning, Sarah. How are you feeling today?" she asked, her voice gentle, inviting conversation rather than demanding it.

I took a deep breath, feeling the weight of the words I was about to speak. "I'm... struggling," I admitted, my voice a mere whisper, yet it felt like a shout in the quiet of the room. "Every day is a battle with memories and what-ifs."

Dr. Ellis nodded, her expression one of

understanding. "It's a difficult journey, Sarah. But you're making progress, even by just being here and talking about it."

The sessions with Dr. Ellis became my lifeline, the one place where I could unravel the tangled web of my emotions without fear of judgment. She guided me gently, helping me to confront the pain of losing Michael, to face the guilt and the regrets that had become my constant companions.

"There are moments," I confessed during one session, "when I feel like I'm drowning in the grief. Like it's this vast ocean, and I'm just... floating, aimless and lost."

"It's normal to feel that way after such a loss," Dr. Ellis replied. "Grief can be overwhelming, but remember, it's also a testament to the depth of your connection with Michael."

As the days passed, I began to peel back the layers of my grief, each revelation a small step toward understanding and acceptance. I talked about Michael, about our moments together, the dreams we had shared, and the stark reality of a future without him. My voice would tremble as I spoke, but with each word, I felt a slight loosening of the grief's hold on me.

"It feels like I'm betraying him by moving on," I said in one session, the words heavy with guilt.

"Sarah, moving forward isn't a betrayal. It's a way of honoring your time with Michael and the impact he had on your life," Dr. Ellis reassured me, her words a beacon in the fog of my sorrow.

These sessions, though painful, became a cathartic release. They were a space where I could lay bare my soul, where I could cry, reminisce, and even laugh without fear. Slowly, I began to see glimmers of hope amidst the despair, like rays of sunlight piercing through a stormy sky.

In therapy, I wasn't just confronting my grief; I was rediscovering myself, learning to navigate a world that had changed irrevocably. It was a journey of healing, of finding strength in my vulnerability and learning to carry the memories of Michael not as a burden, but as a part of who I was becoming.

As I left Dr. Ellis' office after each session, I felt a little lighter, a little more like the Sarah I used to be, yet also someone new - someone who had faced the depths of despair and was slowly, tentatively, finding her way back to the light.

In the bustling atmosphere of the hospital's cafeteria, amid the clatter of trays and the murmur of conversations, I found myself embarking on another crucial aspect of my journey - regaining control over my physical health. The food plan, a structured roadmap of meals, was no longer a chore but a stepping stone toward reclaiming my well-being.

I remember sitting at a corner table, a plate of food in front of me. It was a simple meal - grilled chicken, steamed vegetables, and a small portion of rice. A few weeks ago, the sight of it would have left me indifferent, but now, it represented something more - a conscious choice towards healing.

"You're doing great, Sarah," Nurse Reynolds said one day, as she passed by my table. Her smile was genuine, an acknowledgment of the small yet significant victories I was achieving.

"Thanks," I replied, offering a small smile of my own. It felt good to eat, to feel the nourishment in my body. Each bite was a testament to my growing commitment to get better, to not let grief consume me entirely.

As days turned into weeks, this commitment began to manifest physically. The mirror in my room, once a reminder of my neglect, now reflected a healthier version of myself. My skin regained its color, no longer the pale, lifeless shade it had been. My eyes, which had once looked dull and listless, now held a hint of their former brightness.

It was a slow transformation, each day a step towards a stronger me. I began to feel more energetic, the perpetual fatigue that had weighed me down gradually lifting. My movements, once sluggish, became more purposeful, a reflection of the growing vitality within.

This change was not just about the physical. It was deeply intertwined with my mental recovery. With each meal, I was not only nourishing my body but also feeding my soul, rebuilding myself from the inside out.

The dining hall, once a place I associated with a routine and necessary task, became a space where I could see my progress, where I could feel a part of the community again. I started to join conversations, to connect with others over meals. These interactions were small, often trivial, but they were steps towards rejoining the world around me.

In this part of my journey, I learned the importance of taking care of myself, of honoring my body as much as my mind. It was a lesson in balance, in understanding that healing was a holistic process, encompassing every aspect of my being.

As I continued to follow the food plan, to take those small, deliberate steps towards recovery, I felt a growing sense of hope. It was a quiet, steady flame, burning away the remnants of despair and lighting the path forward. In the simple act of eating, of caring for myself, I was slowly but surely finding my way back to life, to a world where grief did not define my existence, and where the future held possibilities yet to be discovered.

The day Dr. Ellis gently broached the subject of my discharge, the walls of her office seemed to close in around me. "Sarah, you've made remarkable progress," she said, her voice a mix of professionalism and genuine care. "We think you're ready to start transitioning out of the hospital."

Her words, meant to be a recognition of my healing, instead stirred a tempest of emotions within me. The hospital, with its sterile corridors and muted colors, had become more than just a place of recovery; it had become a sanctuary, a repository of the last memories I had of Michael.

In the days following the announcement, I found

myself wandering through the hospital, visiting the spots that Michael and I had frequented. The small bench in the garden where we used to sit became an altar of reflection. I sat there, lost in memories, the ghost of his laughter echoing in my ears.

Each place was a tangible connection to him, to the moments we shared. The quiet corner in the library, the dimly lit hallway where we exchanged secret smiles, the game room where we had our last conversation - each was a thread in the tapestry of our time together.

Leaving these memories behind felt like leaving a part of myself. I grappled with the bittersweet realization that to move forward, I had to let go, not of Michael, but of the hospital that had become a symbol of our connection.

"I'm scared, Dr. Ellis," I confessed during one of our sessions. "This place... it's where I last felt close to him. I'm afraid that leaving means losing that connection."

Dr. Ellis listened, her expression empathetic. "Sarah, the memories you have of Michael aren't confined to these walls. They're a part of you, and they'll stay with you, wherever you go."

Her words were a gentle reminder that healing

meant not just clinging to the past but also embracing the future. It was a daunting thought, stepping out into a world without Michael, but it was also a necessary one.

As I packed my belongings, a mix of emotions swirled within me. Each item I placed in the bag I was given to pack my things felt like closing a chapter, a symbolic act of moving on. The photos of Michael and me, the books we shared, the small trinkets that held our memories - they were all coming with me, a bridge between my past at the hospital and my future beyond its doors.

The night before my discharge, I lay in bed, the moon casting a soft glow through the window. The familiar sounds of the hospital, the distant conversations, the soft footsteps of night staff, were comforting, yet they also underscored the reality of my departure.

I realized then that healing wasn't a destination; it was a journey, one that didn't end with leaving the hospital. It was a path that I would continue to walk, with its ups and downs, its moments of sadness and hope. And as I closed my eyes, a sense of resolve settled in my heart.

Leaving the hospital was not just an end; it was a beginning, a step towards a life where the memories of Michael would be a source of strength, not just of sorrow. It was time to step forward, carrying those memories with me, into a future that was waiting to be written.

The day Ms. Henderson, my social worker, came to visit, the sun was streaming through the windows of the common room, casting a warm glow on the faded walls. But the brightness outside couldn't penetrate the apprehension that had settled over me like a dark cloud.

"Sarah, how are you feeling about your discharge?" Ms. Henderson asked, her tone gentle as she sat across from me, her folder resting on her lap.

I fidgeted with the hem of my shirt, struggling to articulate the turmoil inside me. "I don't know," I replied, my voice barely above a whisper. "It's a lot to process."

Ms. Henderson nodded, her expression understanding. "I know it's a big step, but we've found a foster home for you. The family is very experienced and supportive."

The words 'foster home' sent a ripple of fear through me. The idea of moving into a new, unfamiliar place, with people I didn't know, felt overwhelming. "I'm just not sure if I can handle another change right now," I admitted, the fear evident in my trembling voice.

Ms. Henderson leaned forward slightly, her eyes meeting mine. "I understand your concerns, Sarah. But this is a positive step towards regaining independence. We wouldn't make this decision if we didn't believe you were ready."

I looked down at my hands, feeling a knot of anxiety in my stomach. The thought of leaving the hospital, the only place I had felt safe since Michael's death, was daunting. "What if it doesn't work out?" I asked, the question laden with all the fears and doubts that had been plaguing me.

"We'll be here to support you every step of the way," Ms. Henderson reassured me. "And remember, you've made significant progress here. It's time to apply what you've learned in a new environment."

Her words were meant to be comforting, but they couldn't quell the apprehension that gnawed at me. The hospital had become my sanctuary, a place of healing and reflection. Stepping out of it meant facing a world that had continued to move on without me, a world where Michael no longer existed.

As Ms. Henderson continued to explain the details of the foster home, my mind wandered. I thought about the new family, the new house, and the new routines. Each detail added to the growing sense of unease within me.

The meeting ended with Ms. Henderson offering a final, encouraging smile. "You're stronger than you think, Sarah. This is just another step in your journey."

But as I watched her leave, the reassurance she offered felt distant and hollow. The prospect of moving into a new foster home, of starting over again, was a path shrouded in uncertainty and fear. It was a leap into the unknown, and I wasn't sure if I was ready to take it.

The night before my discharge, I found myself wandering the now-familiar hallways of the hospital, each step echoing against the bright white walls. This place, which had once felt so confining, now seemed like a cocoon, sheltering me from the uncertainties of the outside world. It was here, in these corridors, that I had last felt the presence of Michael, his laughter still lingering like a ghost in the air.

As I passed the garden where we used to sit, the moonlight cast a silver glow over the empty benches, and memories flooded in unbidden. I paused, the cool night air brushing against my skin, bringing with it a wave of longing. "This is where we said goodbye," I whispered to the empty garden, my voice tinged with sorrow.

The hospital had been a witness to our story, to the joy and the pain, to the very last moments we shared. Leaving felt like an abandonment, a betrayal of the memories that were etched into every corner of this place.

But as I stood there, lost in the past, a small voice inside me spoke of the future, of the need to heal and move forward. It was a quiet voice, easily drowned out by the louder echoes of grief, but it was persistent. "You can't stay here forever, Sarah," it seemed to say. "There's a life waiting for you out there."

I returned to my room, my heart heavy with the weight of my impending departure. Lying in my bed, I stared at the ceiling, the shadows playing across it like the conflicting emotions that played across my heart. The comfort and safety of the hospital were all I had known in the wake of Michael's death, and the thought of leaving it behind was daunting.

Yet, amid the fear and uncertainty, there was a flicker of something else - a desire to reclaim my life, to find a path that led beyond grief and sorrow. It was a fragile hope, easily shattered by doubt, but it was there, nonetheless.

"I don't know if I'm ready," I confessed to Nurse Reynolds the next morning, my words heavy with unspoken fears.

She gave me a reassuring smile, her hand resting gently on my shoulder. "It's normal to feel scared, Sarah. But you're stronger than you realize. And remember, you're not alone in this. We're all here for you."

Her words were a balm, but they couldn't entirely soothe the turmoil within me. As I packed my few belongings, each item felt like a piece of the life I was leaving behind - a book I had read in the garden, a sketch I had drawn in a moment of peace, a photo of Michael and me, smiling without a care in the world.

Stepping out of the hospital, the sunlight felt harsh, a stark contrast to the soft glow of the moon in the garden the night before. The world outside seemed too bright, too loud, a sensory overload after the muted existence I had lived for so long.

In the car, as the hospital receded into the distance, I watched it disappear with a sense of loss that was almost physical. It was like watching the last vestige of my old life vanish, leaving me adrift in a new, uncharted reality.

But beneath the fear and the sorrow, there was a thread of courage, however thin. It was the courage to face the unknown, to step into a new chapter of my life, one where the memories of Michael would be a source of strength, not just of pain.

As the car turned onto the highway, I took a deep breath, feeling the finality of the moment. I was leaving the hospital behind, but I was also leaving behind a version of myself. Ahead lay a road filled with uncertainty, but also with possibility. It was time to find out where it led.

13 SABOTAGING STABILITY

The journey through the foster care system felt like navigating a minefield blindfolded. Each new home I entered carried a fragile hope, like a flickering candle in a vast darkness. But the shadows of my past were always lurking, ready to snuff out any glimmer of stability.

The next home was a suburban house with a neatly trimmed lawn and a welcoming porch. The foster parents, Mr. and Mrs. Jenkins, greeted me with cautious optimism. Mr. Jenkins' presence, however, set off alarm bells in my mind. His stature, the way he moved, even his voice, stirred memories best left forgotten.

I remember sitting at their dinner table, Mr. Jenkins' attempts at friendly conversation feeling like an invisible noose tightening around my neck. "So, Sarah, we heard you like to write," he said, passing the salt across the table.

I couldn't respond, my throat constricted with unspoken fears. The meal passed in a tense silence, my every instinct screaming to flee. That night, I lay awake in the guest room, the shadows casting ominous shapes on the walls, each one morphing into a reminder of the dangers that men could pose.

In the weeks that followed, I became a ghost in their home. I avoided Mr. Jenkins at all costs, my interactions with Mrs. Jenkins brief and perfunctory. The strain became palpable, an unspoken tension that hung heavy in the air.

One evening, during a particularly tense dinner, Mrs. Jenkins' patience frayed. "Sarah, we're trying to make you feel at home, but you need to make an effort too," she said, her voice tinged with frustration.

I snapped, my voice cold and distant. "This isn't home. It will never be." The words were a barrier, a defense against the vulnerability that threatened to consume me.

The placement at the Jenkins' home ended soon after, my inability to assimilate into their family dynamic proving too great a hurdle.

The next home was different, a quieter setting with a single foster mother, Ms. Langley. She was kind, but her kindness felt like a trap, luring me into a sense of false security. I responded by withdrawing entirely, barricading myself in my room, refusing to interact.

Ms. Langley tried to reach out, her gentle knocks on my door accompanied by soft words of encouragement. "Sarah, I know this is hard, but I'm here for you. Let's talk when you're ready," she would say, her voice a soothing balm that I stubbornly refused to acknowledge.

My stay with Ms. Langley was marked by a silent rebellion, a refusal to engage with the world she offered. The days blurred into a monotonous cycle of isolation and introspection, the walls of my room becoming the boundaries of my universe.

Each foster home I sabotaged was a testament to the turmoil within me. I was fighting a battle against unseen enemies, haunted by the fear of more abuse, more loss. My actions were a shield, a way to protect myself from the pain of attachment, from the vulnerability that came with trusting others.

But with each disrupted placement, the realization grew that I was not just running from them; I was running from myself, from the trauma that clung to me like a second skin. I was a ship adrift in a stormy sea, my compass spinning wildly, unable to find a course to calmer waters.

As I lay in bed each night, staring into the darkness, I couldn't help but wonder if there was a place out there where I could feel safe, where the shadows of my past wouldn't reach. The answer seemed as elusive as the peace I so desperately sought, a distant dream fading with each passing day.

Next came a seemingly hopeful placement. The Fisher farm was a picturesque sprawl of green fields and rustic charm, a stark contrast to the clinical environment of the hospital or previous homes. When I first arrived, the open spaces and the gentle rhythm of farm life offered a sense of tranquility I hadn't felt in a long time. Mrs. Fisher, with her warm smile and gentle demeanor, reminded me of a mother figure I had longed for.

Amy, with her long bleach blonde curls cascading down her back, greeted me at the door. Her bright blue eyes sparkled with the same warmth as her ever-present smile, instantly lightening the atmosphere. She exuded a friendliness that was both comforting and genuine, embodying a kindred spirit to Mrs. Fisher, with whom she shared a visibly close bond. Amy was a couple years younger than me and had been in the Fisher's home for several years. She seemed to fit right in with the family.

I remember the afternoons spent helping Mrs. Fisher with the cows, her hands expertly guiding mine as we spread hay and cleaned the troughs. "Caring for animals is like therapy," she would say, her voice soft and melodic. "It teaches us patience and the beauty of nurturing."

Amy and I would spend evenings sitting on the porch, talking about everything and nothing or up in her bedroom listening to Eminem while rapping along. In her company, I found a sense of normalcy, a fleeting escape from the ghosts that haunted me.

But this semblance of peace shattered one evening during dinner. The tension had been building for days with Laura, another foster sister, who seemed to harbor resentment towards me. That night, her anger boiled over. "You're just a charity case," she spat, her words laced with venom. "And Michael, he's burning in hell for what he did."

Her cruel words cut through me like a knife, igniting a firestorm of grief and rage. I stood up abruptly, my chair crashing to the floor. "Don't you dare speak about him like that," I yelled, my voice raw with emotion.

I stormed out of the kitchen, my whole body trembling with anger and pain. In my room, the fury simmered, festering into a dark plot of retaliation. Consumed by a desire to make Laura pay, I waited until the house was quiet, the soft snores of its inhabitants the only sound in the night.

Creeping into Laura's room, I unscrewed the cap of the bleach bottle, my hands steady despite the chaos in my heart. As I approached her bed, every step felt like a descent into a darker part of myself.

But as the bleach touched her hair, Laura woke up screaming. The chemical burned her eyes and skin, her cries echoing through the house, a siren of my unforgivable act.

Panic seized me, and I ran back to my room, my heart racing with fear and regret. I knew I had crossed a line, a point of no return. The consequences of my actions were immediate and severe.

Mrs. Fisher's voice was a mix of disbelief and sorrow when she found me. "Sarah, why?" she asked, her eyes searching mine for an answer I couldn't give.

"I don't know," I whispered, the truth more complex than words could express. I had allowed my anger and grief to control me, to drive me to an act of spiteful vengeance.

As I packed my belongings, the reality of what I had done weighed heavily on me. The farm, which had been a haven, was now just another place marked by my turmoil. Leaving it behind, I felt a deep sense of loss, not just for the comfort it had offered, but for the part of me that I had lost in the darkness of my anger.

The car ride to the secured residential group home was a blur, my mind reeling from the events of the night. I was stepping into a new chapter, one that held the promise of structure and support, but also the fear of confronting the deeper issues that had driven me to such destructive behavior.

As the car pulled up to the group home, a sturdy building with a fenced yard, I took a deep breath. This was a new beginning, a chance to face my demons in a space designed to help me heal. But as I stepped out of the car, I couldn't shake the feeling of apprehension, the fear of what lay ahead in this latest twist in my journey.

There it stood, stark and imposing, its structured facade a symbol of the new chapter I was about to begin. As I stepped through its doors, a mix of hope and apprehension churned within me. The walls, painted a neutral shade, and the orderly arrangement of the common areas spoke of a regimented environment, designed to provide stability for those like me, grappling with complex emotional turmoil.

Ms. Carter, the home's supervisor, greeted me with a firm handshake. "Welcome, Sarah. We're here to support you," she said, her voice a blend of authority and kindness. Her words were meant to reassure, but they echoed in the hollow space of my uncertainty.

My room, resembling more of a jail cell, had a barred window that looked out onto a small, fenced garden. The thin bed was neatly made, and the few shelves were empty. A stark reminder that this was yet another temporary stop in my tumultuous journey.

As night fell on my first day, I sat on the edge of my bed, the events of the past weeks replaying in my mind like a haunting melody. The bleach incident at the farm, the pain and fear in Laura's eyes, the look of disappointment on Mrs. Fisher's face - each memory was a sharp stab of regret.

I knew my actions were wrong, driven by a maelstrom of unresolved grief and anger. Yet, understanding the root of my behavior didn't lessen the weight of guilt that pressed down on me. It was a burden I carried, a constant reminder of the pain I had caused, both to others and to myself.

Lying in bed, the darkness of the room enveloping me, my thoughts drifted to Michael. Laura's cruel words about him echoed in my head, igniting a fresh wave of sorrow and fear. The idea of him suffering, of being punished for the way he died, was unbearable.

I tossed and turned, trying to escape the unnerving thoughts, but they clung to me, persistent and unyielding. The silence of the room was oppressive, broken only by the sound of my own uneven breathing.

Sleep felt like an impossible dream, a respite just out of reach. Every time I closed my eyes, Michael's face appeared, his eyes filled with the pain and confusion of our last moments together. The fear of falling asleep, of sinking into nightmares that I couldn't control, kept me awake, my eyes fixed on the shadowy ceiling.

In this new environment, surrounded by strangers and rules, I felt more alone than ever. The group home, with its promise of support and structure, also felt like a cage, a place where my freedom to grieve and heal was confined within strict boundaries.

As the clock ticked slowly towards morning, the realization dawned that this was just the beginning of a new struggle. Here, in the quiet of my locked room, I had to confront not only the memories of what I had lost but also the daunting task of rebuilding myself.

The path ahead was unclear, shrouded in fear and uncertainty. But despite the apprehension that gripped me, a small part of me clung to the hope that maybe, just maybe, this place could be the start of a journey towards true healing, towards finding a peace that had eluded me since Michael's death.

As dawn's first light crept into the room, casting a soft glow on the stark walls, I made a silent vow to try, to take each day as it came, and to face the challenges ahead. But for now, in the quiet before the day began, I lay there, a lone figure in a room filled with the ghosts of the past and the daunting shadows of the future.

14 A DANCE WITH FATE

The first rays of morning light seeped through the narrow window, casting long, shadowy fingers across the already gloomy room. I lay there, in my narrow bed, feeling the weight of the new day settling upon me. The Secured residential group home, with its unyielding routines and cold, prison-like atmosphere, pressed down on me like a heavy blanket, stifling any remnants of the freedom I once cherished.

I pushed myself out of bed, the metallic frame creaking under my weight. The room felt smaller in the daylight, the walls closing in, painted in a lifeless shade that reminded me of hospital corridors. The air was stale, carrying a faint antiseptic smell that seemed to strip away any sense of home or comfort.

As I heard the door unlock, I made my way to the dining area. The clatter of utensils and the low hum of conversations filled the space, but none of it seemed welcoming. As I took a seat, I felt the oppressive gaze of the staff members, their eyes scanning the room like hawks. Their presence was a constant reminder of the control they wielded over us.

I attempted to engage in small talk with a resident seated across from me. "How long have you been here?" I asked, my voice barely above a whisper.

She glanced up, her eyes hollow, shadowed. "Too long," she muttered before returning her gaze to her untouched plate.

The conversation, if it could be called that, died there. I poked at my food, the blandness of the oatmeal matching the dreariness of my surroundings. Around me, conversations were hushed, as if everyone was afraid of drawing attention to themselves.

A staff member, Ms. Jenkins, approached our table, her footsteps echoing on the linoleum floor. "Eat up, everyone. You'll need your strength for today's activities," she announced, though her tone lacked any real warmth.

I looked up at her, trying to read her expression. Was there a hint of compassion in her eyes, or was it merely a reflection of her duty?

I swallowed a spoonful of oatmeal, the lump of it heavy in my throat. It felt like I was swallowing my words, my thoughts, my very being, conforming to the rigid structure that now dictated my life.

Ms. Jenkins lingered for a moment, her eyes scanning the room before moving on. As she walked away, I couldn't help but feel a prickling sensation at the back of my neck, a silent warning of the watchful eyes always upon us.

Breakfast continued in silence, each of us isolated in our own thoughts, trapped not just by the walls of the group home but also by the barriers we had erected within ourselves. It was as if we were all dancing a careful, choreographed routine, one wrong step away from chaos.

As I left the dining area, I felt a sense of foreboding settling in my chest. This was just the beginning, the first day of many in this place where every move was monitored, every emotion scrutinized. The group home was not just a facility; it was a test of endurance, a dance with fate where each step could either lead to salvation or further descent into the abyss of despair.

As the clock struck noon, the tension in my body had ratcheted up to an almost unbearable level. The morning's oppressive silence and the weight of watchful eyes had festered into a simmering anger within me. The lunchroom, with its rows of plain tables and the monotonous clatter of cutlery, felt like another stage for our puppet show – everyone playing their part in this controlled chaos.

I stood in line, tray in hand, mechanically accepting the portions doled out by the staff. The food was as bland and uninspiring as the surroundings, each item a reminder of the rigid control exerted over every aspect of our lives here.

Sitting down at a table, I could feel the staff's eyes boring into me, their presence a suffocating blanket. The murmurs around me were a low hum, a soundtrack to the collective resignation that seemed to hang in the air.

Then, it happened.

A staff member, Mr. Thompson, approached our table. "Remember, lights out by nine tonight. No exceptions," he announced, his voice carrying an authoritative edge.

Something inside me snapped. "Why nine? Why can't we have some say in this?" I shot back, my voice louder than I had intended.

The lunchroom fell into a sudden hush, all eyes turning to our table. Mr. Thompson's face hardened. "Rules are rules, Sarah. They're in place for your safety and well-being."

"Safety? It feels more like a prison!" I stood up, my chair scraping loudly against the floor. My heart was pounding, anger and frustration boiling over.

"This isn't a discussion. Sit down," Mr. Thompson ordered, his tone brooking no argument.

But I was past caring. "No, I won't. We're not just inmates here. We're people, and we deserve some control over our lives!"

Mr. Thompson stepped closer, his stance rigid. "That's enough, Sarah. This behavior won't be tolerated."

The defiance in me had taken full control. "What will you do? Lock me up for speaking my mind?"

Before I could react, two other staff members appeared at my side. They grabbed my arms, their grip firm and unyielding. I struggled against them, a mix of fear and anger fueling my resistance.

"Let me go!" I yelled, trying to shake them off. But

their hold only tightened.

"We're taking you back to your room. You need to calm down," one of them said, his voice a cold, impersonal drone.

As they dragged me away, the eyes of the other residents followed, a silent audience to my rebellion and its swift suppression. My heart raced, a chaotic drumbeat echoing my tumultuous thoughts.

The realization hit me then – in my attempt to fight against the system, I had only ensnared myself further. This place, with its suffocating rules and watchful eyes, was not just a group home; it was a battleground for the spirit, and I had just lost another skirmish in the ongoing war for my sense of self.

In the solitude of my room, the four walls felt more like the confines of a cell than ever before. I sat on the edge of my bed, the aftermath of my outburst still echoing in my ears. The silence was oppressive, suffocating, filled with the weight of words unsaid and actions undone.

My mind wandered, unbidden, to my last conversation with my foster sister. The memory was vivid, her words slicing through me with renewed sharpness "And Michael, he's burning in hell for what he did."

Michael, my anchor in a sea of turmoil, gone forever. The thought of him in hell, suffering eternally, was more than I could bear. Tears welled up in my eyes, spilling over in silent sobs. The pain of loss mingled with the helplessness I felt in this place, creating a maelstrom of grief and despair.

I lay down, my body wracked with sobs, the wetness of my tears soaking the pillow. As exhaustion overtook me, my thoughts spiraled into darkness, and I slipped into an uneasy sleep.

In my dream, the world was distorted, a landscape of shadows and whispers. I was in a place that resembled the group home, but it was twisted, nightmarish. The walls pulsed with a life of their own, and the air was thick with a sense of foreboding.

I heard Michael's voice, distant and distorted, as if through water. "Sarah, why did you let me go?"

I ran through the hallways, trying to find him, but with each step, the corridors grew longer, more labyrinthine. His voice was a beacon, guiding yet eluding me.

Then, I saw him, standing at the end of a long, dark hallway. He was backlit, his features obscured, a silhouette of the boy I loved. "Michael!" I cried, my voice echoing in the empty space.

But as I approached, he began to fade, like mist in the morning sun. "I'm here, Sarah. But you're not. You let me go," his voice was a haunting whisper, filled with pain and accusation.

I reached out, desperately trying to touch him, to hold onto something, anything. But my hands grasped only air. "I didn't! I couldn't save you," I sobbed, the words torn from the depths of my soul.

The dream shifted, and I was now standing in a void, alone. Michael's voice was a fading echo, a reminder of all that I had lost. "You're alone, Sarah. You couldn't save me. You can't even save yourself."

I woke up with a start, my heart racing, a thin sheen of sweat covering my skin. The remnants of the dream clung to me, a shroud of fear and guilt. The darkness of my room felt oppressive, a tangible manifestation of my nightmare.

Lying there, in the cold and uninviting room, I realized that my grief for Michael was more than just sorrow for his passing. It was a reflection of my own fears, my own sense of powerlessness in a world that seemed to be slipping further and further from my grasp. Each day in this residential group home, each rule, each controlled interaction, was a reminder that I was no longer the master of my own fate.

In the depths of my despair, I understood that my struggle wasn't just against the walls of the group home, but against the barriers within myself. The barriers of fear, of loss, of guilt that held me captive far more effectively than any lock and key.

The haunting remnants of my nightmare lingered as I lay there in the bright light of my room, the afternoon sun still creeping through the small window. My heart was racing, each beat a loud drum in the overwhelming silence. The walls seemed to close in on me, the air thick with the weight of my despair.

I sat up, a sense of desperation clawing at my chest. The grief for Michael, the oppressive environment of the group home, the loss of my freedom – it all converged into a singular, unbearable point of pain. I felt trapped, not just within these walls, but within my own mind, a prisoner to my fears and sorrows.

In that moment, a desperate thought took root. I wanted to escape, to free myself from this endless cycle of pain. The idea was terrifying, yet it held a promise of release.

With trembling hands, I took the thin sheet from my bed. My movements were mechanical, driven by a force beyond my understanding. I twisted the sheet into a makeshift noose, the fabric coarse against my skin.

There was a beam on the ceiling, part of the room's stark, utilitarian design. I stood on a chair, my heart pounding in my ears, the sheet in my hands. As I tied the noose around the beam, my mind was a whirlwind of emotion – fear, despair, a desperate longing for peace.

I placed the noose around my neck, the fabric feeling like ice against my skin. My breath was shallow, each inhalation a sharp intake of the cold, sterile air of the room.

And then, I stepped off the chair.

In that instant, as I dangled, suspended between life and death, a flood of dread and regret washed over me. The reality of what I had done, the finality of it, struck me with a force that left me breathless.

I reached out, my fingers grasping for the chair, but it was just out of reach. Panic set in, a wild, clawing thing that screamed for survival. "No, no, no," I gasped, the words a choked whisper.

My vision began to blur, the edges of the room fading into darkness. My thoughts were a jumble of fear and desperation. I wanted to live, I realized. Despite the pain, despite the despair, I wanted to live.

But the noose was tight, unyielding, and the room was slipping away. My last thoughts were filled with regret, a silent plea for a second chance, a cry for help that seemed to echo in the void.

Then, through the encroaching darkness, I heard a sound. A distant scream, the noise of the door being unlocked in haste. The last thing I saw before consciousness slipped away was the door swinging open, the figure of a staff member, their face a blur of motion and fear.

In that moment, as the world faded to black, I realized the tragic irony of my act. In seeking to escape my pain, I had only found a deeper despair, a more profound fear. It was a lesson learned too late, a realization that came at the cost of everything.

Consciousness returned to me like a reluctant tide, ebbing in with a cacophony of sounds and a flurry of sensations. I lay there, disoriented, the stark white lights of the hospital room blinding me. Voices swirled around me, distant yet insistent, puncturing the fog that enveloped my mind.

"You're back with us, Sarah," a gentle voice said, a hand squeezing mine. I blinked, trying to bring the world into focus. A nurse stood beside me, her expression a blend of relief and concern.

I tried to speak, but my throat was raw, each word a painful scrape. "What... happened?" My voice was barely audible, a hoarse whisper.

The nurse offered a small, sad smile. "You had a very close call. But you're safe now. You're in the hospital."

The words sank in slowly, the reality of what I had done - and what had almost happened - dawning on me. I had been so consumed by despair, so blinded by pain, that I had nearly ended my own life. The regret was a tangible thing, a heavy weight in my chest.

I looked around the room, taking in the sterile environment, the beeping machines, the IV drip attached to my arm. This place, with its clinical efficiency, was a sharp difference to the chaos and turmoil of my inner world.

The nurse continued to speak, her voice soft yet firm. "Sarah, what you did... it was a serious thing. We're here to help you, but you need to be honest with us. Can you do that?"

I nodded, a lump forming in my throat. "I... I don't know why I did it. I was just so tired of everything."

"It's okay to feel overwhelmed," the nurse said. "But there are people who care about you, who want to help you through this."

Her words were a small comfort, a lifeline in the stormy sea of my thoughts. I realized then that my journey was far from over. The road to healing, to understanding myself and dealing with my pain, was going to be long and difficult.

As the nurse left the room, promising to return soon, I lay there, staring at the ceiling. The events of the day replayed in my mind, each moment a sharp stab of regret. I had come so close to ending my story, to cutting short the narrative of my life.

This chapter of my life, marked by despair and a near-tragic decision, was a pivotal one. It underscored the fragility of my existence within these institutional walls, the delicate balance between holding on and letting go. It was a stark reminder of the need for support, for understanding, and for a compassionate hand to guide me through the darkest moments of my journey.

In the silence of the room, with the steady beep of the heart monitor as my only company, I made a silent vow to myself. I would try to find the strength to continue, to face the pain and the fear head-on. It wouldn't be easy, but perhaps, in time, I could find a way to navigate through the chaos and find a semblance of peace.

The journey ahead was uncertain, filled with potential pitfalls and challenges, but it was mine to take. And for the first time in a long while, I felt a flicker of hope amidst the despair, a small yet persistent flame that refused to be extinguished.

15 RETURN TO THE STATE HOSPITAL

The familiar, sterile scent of the state hospital hits me the moment I cross its threshold. It's a smell that's hard to describe—part disinfectant, part despair. I've walked through these doors more times than I care to count, but each time feels like a surrender, a step back into a world where I don't belong.

I pause, my heart sinking further with each reluctant step I take inside. The nurse's desk is just as I remember it: bland, with faded posters about mental health plastered on the walls. It's as if the place is stuck in time, frozen in its own unchanging routine.

The staff don't even try to hide their annoyance as they recognize me. "Back again, Sarah?" one of them mutters, her voice dripping with a weariness that mirrors my own. They don't say it, but their eyes do—their looks of thinly veiled frustration, their dismissive glances. I'm an inconvenience, a problem they thought they had gotten rid of.

I clench my fists, feeling the sting of their judgment like a physical slap. "Yeah, back again," I reply, my voice steady despite the turmoil inside. I've learned to mask my feelings, to hide the hurt behind a façade of indifference. But it's getting harder each time.

As I wait for the check-in process, the familiar sounds of the hospital fill the air—the distant chatter of staff members, the occasional beep from a door locking, the soft shuffle of slippers against the linoleum floor. It's a rhythm of despair, a melody that speaks of broken minds and shattered spirits.

I'm escorted down the hallway, my steps slow, each one heavier than the last. The walls are lined with doors, each leading to a room that holds a story, a life put on pause. My room is like every time before, stark and uninviting. A single bed, a small window, a desk with nothing on it. It's a space void of personality, a place where hope seems to wither.

I sit on the edge of the bed, the mattress barely yielding under my weight. The room feels smaller than I remember, or maybe I'm just more aware of the confines that surround me. I look out the window, the view limited to a small patch of sky and the top of a tree. It's a glimpse of a world that feels increasingly out of reach.

"Sarah, you need to take your medication," Nurse Brown says, her voice interrupting my thoughts. She's holding a small cup filled with pills, the colors and shapes all too familiar.

I shake my head, my resolve firm. "I'm not taking them. Not this time." The words are a challenge, a small act of rebellion in a place where I have little control.

She sighs, her patience thin. "You know the drill, Sarah. You don't have a choice."

But I do have a choice. It's the one thing I cling to—the knowledge that, in this small way, I can still defy them. I can still fight.

The nurse leaves, her footsteps echoing in the empty corridor. I'm left alone, the silence a heavy blanket that wraps around me. In this moment, I'm both a prisoner and a rebel, caught in a battle that seems endless.

And so, I brace myself for what's to come, the familiar cycle of defiance and discipline. It's a dance I know all too well, each step leading me further into the depths of this place—a place that's supposed to heal but only seems to break me more.

But I won't give in. Not completely. There's a part of me that refuses to be crushed, a spirit that still fights, even in the face of overwhelming despair. It's the part of me that keeps me going, the flicker of hope that refuses to be extinguished.

I storm out of my room, my heart pounding in my chest. The game room is my destination, a place where I can hide, at least for a little while. The walls of the hallway seem to close in on me as I walk, each step a rebellion, a statement of my refusal to be controlled.

Inside the game room, I find a momentary sanctuary. The sound of a television playing some mindless show, the clatter of board game pieces being moved around a table by indifferent hands, it's all background noise. My mind is racing, a whirlwind of anger and defiance.

But my respite is short-lived. The sound of heavy footsteps approaches, and I know it's security. They're here for me. I don't need to turn around to know their faces are set in grim determination. This isn't their first time, and it's not mine either.

"Sarah, you need to come with us," one of the guards says, his voice firm but not unkind.

I whirl around, my anger boiling over. "I'm not

going anywhere with you!" My voice is loud, too loud, echoing off the walls of the room.

The other patients look up, their eyes wide with a mix of curiosity and excitement. I don't want an audience, but I can't back down now. Not when everything inside me is screaming to fight, to resist.

The guards move towards me, their movements deliberate. I can see it in their eyes, the resignation, the weariness. They've done this too many times, but so have I.

I lash out, trying to break free from their grip. My fists flail, connecting with nothing but air. It's futile, and I know it, but I can't stop. The fear mixes with my anger, a toxic cocktail that drives me.

They're stronger than me, their hands gripping my arms with a force that's both painful and terrifying. I kick, I scream, I do everything I can to break free, but it's like fighting against a tide.

"Let me go!" I shout, but my voice is lost in the chaos.

The struggle seems to last forever, but it's only minutes. Minutes in which my spirit fights against the inevitable. When they finally drag me out of the game room, I'm exhausted, my body aching, my heart heavy.

I'm taken back to the medication area and feel trapped. The guards' firm grips on my arms feel like iron shackles, unyielding and cold. I can't move; I can't escape. The nurse, with a cup of medication in her hand, steps forward. Her face is a mask of professional detachment, but I can sense the frustration simmering beneath.

"Open your mouth, Sarah," she instructs, a hint of command in her tone.

I clench my teeth, refusing to comply. But the guards are unrelenting. One of them tips my head back, forcing my mouth open. The nurse seizes the opportunity, pouring the contents of the cup into my mouth. Immediately after, she follows with a stream of water, urging, "Swallow it."

The medication and water mix in my mouth, a bitter and vile concoction. Anger surges through me, overpowering any sense of compliance. In a moment of defiance, I spit the mixture right back at her, the droplets landing on her face and uniform.

The nurse recoils, a mix of shock and disgust flashing across her features. "Sarah!" she exclaims, wiping her face with the back of her hand.

I try to break free, but the guards tighten their hold. In the scuffle, we all stumble. Their strength is overwhelming, and I'm forced down to the ground. The impact sends a jolt of pain through my body, and I cry out, but they don't seem to care. They're focused on subduing me, their actions more forceful than necessary.

"Stop resisting!" one of the guards barks, his voice close to my ear.

The nurse kneels beside me, her hands grabbing my arms and pulling them harshly behind my back. The pain is immediate, sharp and burning. Tears spring to my eyes, but I refuse to let them fall. I won't give them the satisfaction of seeing me break.

They lift me off the ground, half-carrying, half-dragging me to the seclusion room. Every step is agony, my shoulders aching from the unnatural angle. I'm fighting every inch of the way, but it's like battling a tide.

The seclusion room feels like a concrete box, cold and unyielding. The door slams shut with a finality that echoes through the small space and into my bones. I'm left alone, but not at peace. The anger inside me, a raging inferno, refuses to be quelled.

I pace the room, each step a drumbeat of frustration.

The walls, stark and bare, seem to close in on me, suffocating me with their indifference. My hands form fists, and I start banging on the door, the sound loud and desperate. "Let me out!" I scream, my voice hoarse with emotion. The words bounce back at me, mocking echoes in the solitary chamber.

But the door doesn't budge. It stands firm, a barrier between me and the world outside. My shouts continue, a litany of rage and despair, but they bring no relief, no response. It's as if I'm screaming into a void.

After what feels like an eternity, the door finally opens. The staff return, their faces set in grim determination. They're here to restrain me, to rob me of even the small freedom of movement I have left.

"No!" I yell as they approach, but my protest falls on deaf ears. They're professionals, trained to deal with situations like this, and I'm just another patient, another problem to be handled.

The struggle is brief but intense. They're too strong, too many, and I'm just one person, one girl fighting against a system that feels designed to break me. They pin me down on the bed, my arms and legs flailing, trying to escape their grasp. But it's futile. The restraints come out, leather straps that are cold and unfeeling against my skin.

As they secure the restraints, I feel a sense of defeat washing over me. My body is confined, but it's my spirit that truly feels trapped. "Why are you doing this?" I plead, but my voice is barely a whisper, lost in the chaos.

One of the staff, a nurse with a syringe in her hand, leans over me. "This will help you calm down," she says, her voice attempting a tone of comfort that feels out of place in this setting.

I want to resist, to fight against the sedative, but I'm so tired, so worn down. The needle pierces my skin, a sharp pinch that's quickly overshadowed by the spreading numbness. My thoughts start to blur, the edges of my anger softening.

I can feel the sedative taking effect, dragging me down into a drowsy haze. My eyelids grow heavy, my mind foggy. The last thing I see before darkness claims me is the ceiling of the seclusion room, a blank canvas that offers no comfort, no escape.

As I slip into unconsciousness, I realize that this is just another battle in a war I've been fighting for too long. A war against myself, against a world that doesn't seem to understand or care. And in this moment, I'm not sure if I'm winning or losing. All I know is that I'm tired, so very tired, of fighting.

16 THE EDGE OF ENDURANCE

In the sterile, monochrome confines of the state hospital, time becomes a meaningless concept, each day bleeding into the next in an unending parade of sameness. After my last sedation, the hours stretch and warp, each one a carbon copy of the one before. In this numbing routine, I fall back to my old form of rebellion in refusing to eat. It's not much, but it's all I have left in a place that tries to strip me of my will, my autonomy.

The staff watch me with an eagle's eye, their response clinical, detached, yet unnervingly precise. They've placed me under strict eating precautions, and there's always someone with me - a constant, oppressive shadow that haunts my every step, even in the most private of spaces. It's a relentless invasion, a stripping away of any shred of dignity I might have clung to.

"Sarah, you need to eat something," the assigned

staff member urges during meal times, their voice a persistent, grating presence. I'm seated alone, a solitary figure with a plate of untouched food before me. Their words blend into a monotonous drone in the background of my mind. I push the plate away, each refusal a tiny triumph in my otherwise powerless existence. They offer me Ensure, the can of liquid sustenance cold and unappealing in my hands, but I just set it aside, my lips sealed shut.

Their vigilance follows me everywhere. In the bathroom, under the harsh, unforgiving lights of the shower, I feel their eyes on me, guarding against any attempt to rid myself of the meager nourishment they've managed to force upon me. It's dehumanizing, this constant surveillance, a relentless intrusion that leaves me feeling exposed and raw.

But then, one day, their patience snaps. I hear the heavy tread of security outside my door, their presence heralding something more sinister. "Sarah, we need to do this. You're not giving us any choice," one of them says, his voice a cold, impersonal timbre.

I resist, pushing against them with a futile desperation. "No! You can't keep doing this to me!" My protests are drowned out by the clinical efficiency of their actions.

They drag me out into the hallway, my struggle on display for anyone to see. The other patients' eyes are on me - some filled with a ghostly sympathy, others turning away, unable to bear witness to my degradation. I'm restrained to a chair right there in the open, the cold leather of the straps biting into my skin.

As the nurse approaches with the feeding tube, my heart pounds against my ribcage. "Please, don't," I whisper, but my plea falls on deaf ears. The tube is forced upon me, a physical and psychological intrusion that's about far more than just food. It's about submission, about breaking my will.

Tears escape my eyes, not from the physical pain but from a deeper, more visceral wound. This isn't just a violation of my body; it's a systematic dismantling of my spirit. As the tube snakes down, I realize that in this place, my struggles, my fights, they're just echoes in a void, unheard and unheeded. And in this moment, I've never felt more helpless.

Over the next few weeks, In the stark, unyielding walls of the hospital, something within me starts to shift. It's subtle at first, like the slow change of seasons, but it's there – a transformation born out of necessity. The relentless cycle of conflict, of force and restraint, has begun to chip away at the foundations of my resilience. I come to realize that my defiance, though cathartic, is nothing more than a Pyrrhic victory, each act of rebellion only serving to prolong my entrapment.

So, with a heart laden with unspoken despair, I embark on a new strategy – feigned compliance. It's not surrender, but a tactical retreat, a way to manipulate the system that seeks to break me.

"Good morning, Sarah," the nurse greets me, her voice carrying the usual note of professional detachment.

"Good morning," I reply, my tone light, and practiced. Every word, every gesture, is a calculated act. I offer a faint smile, one that doesn't quite reach my eyes but serves its purpose.

At mealtimes, I no longer push the food away. Instead, I pick at it, taking small, reluctant bites. It's an act of concession, a performance for the watchful eyes of the staff. I can feel their scrutiny, but I meet it with a mask of cooperation.

"How's the food today?" one of the staff members asks, trying to engage me in conversation.

"It's okay," I respond, keeping my voice neutral,

and agreeable. The truth is the food still tastes like ash in my mouth, but I've learned the art of deception. It's about survival, about navigating this intricate dance between autonomy and subjugation.

My daily routines, once a battleground of wills, become a series of well-rehearsed scenes. I attend therapy sessions, nodding along, offering just enough engagement to satisfy their criteria. The therapists note my 'improvement,' unaware of the façade I've constructed.

In the privacy of my room, though, the mask falls away. I allow myself to feel the full weight of my emotions – the anger, the despair, the gnawing sense of helplessness. But these moments are mine alone, hidden away from the prying eyes of the hospital staff.

Day by day, I continue this charade, a delicate balancing act between outward submission and inner rebellion. It's a game of chess, and I'm slowly, meticulously moving my pieces, biding my time. I know that this isn't a permanent solution, but it's a necessary one.

In this world of clinical walls and watchful eyes, I've learned that sometimes the greatest act of defiance is to hide in plain sight. And so, I wear my mask of compliance like armor, each day a step closer to an escape that I desperately hope is within reach.

My newfound strategy of feigned compliance weaves itself into every interaction, every routine. It's exhausting, this constant act, but I remind myself it's a means to an end.

One morning, as I sit listlessly in the common area, a therapist approaches me. "Sarah, you seem more engaged lately. How are you feeling about your progress?" she asks, her pen poised over her notepad, ready to capture my response.

I look up, meeting her gaze with a carefully neutral expression. "I think I'm starting to understand things better," I reply, my voice a well-rehearsed blend of introspection and hopefulness. Inside, I scoff at the idea of 'progress' in a place that feels more like a prison than a healing environment.

"That's good to hear, Sarah. Remember, we're all here to help you," she responds, her tone sincere yet oblivious to the irony of her words.

In therapy sessions, I offer just enough participation to appear cooperative. "I'm learning to cope with my feelings better," I say during one session, the words feeling foreign as they leave my mouth. The therapist nods approvingly, not seeing the hollow truth behind my eyes.

Even with the staff, I maintain this façade. "Could I please have some more water?" I ask politely, my request mundane yet part of the intricate dance of deception.

"Of course, Sarah. It's good to see you taking care of yourself," the nurse replies, handing me a cup.

Every polite request, every forced bite of food, every nod in therapy – they're all calculated moves in this game of pretense. But as I navigate this new strategy, a part of me fears losing myself in this act, the lines between façade and reality blurring.

Nights are the hardest. Alone in my room, the walls seem to close in, and the weight of my own duplicity threatens to suffocate me. I lie in bed, staring at the ceiling, grappling with the fear that this mask may become my new face, that in my effort to survive, I'll lose the essence of who I am.

But with each passing day, I remind myself why I'm doing this. It's not just about escaping the hospital; it's about reclaiming my life, my choices, my future. And so, I hold on to my plan, to the hope that by playing their game, I might eventually find my way out of this labyrinth of despair.

The days wear on, each one a monotonous echo of the last, until one afternoon, my social worker, Ms. Henderson, arrives. She's a familiar face in the sea of indifference, but today, she carries an air of cautious optimism.

"Sarah, I have some news for you," she begins, sitting down across from me in the small, stark meeting room.

I look up, my heart starting to beat a little faster. News in this place can mean anything. "What is it?" I ask, my voice guarded.

"We've arranged a transfer for you to a new foster home," she reveals, her eyes searching mine for a reaction.

For a moment, her words hang in the air, heavy with implications. A new foster home. The phrase is laden with a mixture of hope and trepidation. Part of me wants to leap at the chance, to embrace the possibility of a fresh start. But another part, the part that's been hurt and disappointed so many times before, holds back, steeped in skepticism.

"A new home?" I echo, my tone laced with a wariness born from experience. "What makes this one any different?"

Ms. Henderson nods, understanding the depth of my hesitation. "I know you've been through a lot, Sarah. But this family, they're experienced with kids who have faced challenges. They're prepared to provide the support you need."

Her words are meant to reassure me, but they stir a familiar fear within me. How many times have I heard similar promises, only to be met with more disappointment?

I take a deep breath, trying to steady the whirlwind of thoughts. "When?" I ask, a part of me still clinging to the fragile thread of hope that this time might be different.

"In a few days," she replies. "We're finalizing the details."

I nod, a silent acknowledgment of the news. As Ms. Henderson continues to talk, outlining the plans, a part of me drifts away. I'm caught in the push and pull of hope and fear, the desire for a new beginning wrestling with the scars of the past.

The meeting ends with Ms. Henderson promising to return soon, and I'm left alone with my thoughts. The room feels smaller, more confining, as if the walls are inching closer, pressing in on me with the weight of what's to come.

I sit there, my gaze unfocused, staring at a point somewhere beyond the confines of the room. A new foster home. The words are a beacon in the darkness, yet I can't shake the fear that it might just be another mirage.

I feel in a state of limbo, caught between the past and the future. The promise of change is on the horizon, a glimmer of light in the perpetual dusk of my life. I just want to go home, with my mother and siblings, but the path ahead is uncertain, shrouded in the shadows of doubt and fear. And as I sit there, alone with my thoughts, I can't help but wonder: will this new home be the sanctuary I've been longing for, will I go home after, or is it just another stop in my seemingly endless journey of survival?

17 TURBULENT TRANSITIONS

The drive to my new foster home seems to drag on forever but eventually, the car pulls up to a quaint house with a neatly trimmed lawn, the kind of place that, under different circumstances, might have felt welcoming. I step out, clutching the trash bag that holds my only belongings – a tangible reminder of the many moves I've endured and their abrupt endings.

My new foster parents are waiting at the door, their smiles wide and seemingly genuine. "Welcome, Sarah! We're so glad to have you here," the woman says, her voice warm.

"Thank you," I respond, my voice barely above a whisper. My eyes scan the surroundings, instinctively searching for signs of what might lie beneath their welcoming façade. Years in the system have taught me that appearances can be deceiving, that smiles often hide more than they reveal.

The man extends his hand. "I'm John, and this is my wife, Linda. We'll do our best to make you feel at home."

I shake his hand, the gesture automatic. "Nice to meet you," I reply, but my words feel hollow, even to my own ears.

They lead me inside, showing me around the house. It's cozy, filled with the trappings of a 'normal' family life, but to me, it feels alien, another temporary stop in my seemingly endless journey.

My new room is upstairs, a stark contrast to the sterile, clinical rooms I've grown accustomed to. The walls are adorned with posters and pictures, expressions of a personality that's supposed to be mine, but isn't. I place my bag on the bed, a small island in a sea of unfamiliarity.

"Take your time settling in," Linda says, her tone kind. "Dinner will be ready soon. We hope you'll join us."

I nod, forcing a small smile. "Sure."

As they leave, closing the door gently behind them, the smile fades from my face. I look around the room, each item a reminder of how out of place I feel. The posters on the walls, the books on the shelf, the soft bedding – they're meant to comfort, but they only serve to heighten my sense of detachment.

I sit on the edge of the bed, my thoughts drifting to the countless rooms I've occupied before this one. Each promised a fresh start, a new beginning, but all they ever led to was more disappointment, more heartache.

The fear and skepticism that have become my normal counterpart rise within me, whispering reminders of past betrayals, of promises broken. I wish I could believe that this time will be different, that this place will finally be the home I've longed for. But experience has taught me to brace for the fall, for the inevitable moment when this, too, will crumble away.

As I unpack my few belongings, a couple outfits that no longer fit well, a hairbrush, a toothbrush, and a book that had been torn, I feel a deep, aching weariness. Between all the moves, anything I had that meant much had been lost or thrown out. I shove them all into the dresser that's way too big for the little that I own and I sit on the edge of the bed feeling defeated. It's the tiredness of a soul that's been tossed about by the storm of life, longing for a shore that always seems just out of reach.

Dinner that evening is an awkward affair. I sit at the table, surrounded by the sounds of a family I am yet to feel part of. John and Linda try to engage me in conversation, their questions gentle, and probing.

"So, Sarah, do you have any hobbies? Anything you like to do in your spare time?" Linda asks, passing me the salad bowl.

I hesitate, unsure how much to reveal, how much to keep hidden. "I... I like reading," I say finally, keeping my gaze fixed on the salad, not wanting to meet her eyes.

"That's wonderful! We have plenty of books around the house," John chimes in, his enthusiasm a stark contrast to my muted tone.

The meal continues with more small talk, the kind of chatter that families engage in, but to me, it sounds like a language I'm yet to learn. I respond when necessary, but mostly, I find myself retreating behind a wall of silence, my mind a whirl of thoughts and emotions.

Later, as I lie in my new bed, the house quiet around me, the events of the day replay in my mind. The polite smiles, the carefully worded questions, the feeling of being an outsider in someone else's home – it's a familiar script, one I've acted in too many times.

As sleep eludes me, I find myself staring at the ceiling, lost in the memories of all the homes I've been in, all the families I've tried to fit into. Each one had promised a new beginning, a chance for something better, but each time, I'd found myself back at square one, packing my bag and moving on.

I think about Michael, his face appearing in my mind's eye, a painful reminder of a loss that still feels raw. And then, there's the looming shadow of my stepfather, his presence a dark cloud that never seems to dissipate.

The night stretches on, and I'm left alone with my thoughts, the ghosts of my past keeping me company. I wonder if this time will be any different, if I'll finally find a place where I belong, or if it's just a matter of time before I'm packing my bag again, moving on to the next temporary stop in my life.

As I drift off to a restless sleep, the uncertainty of the future is a heavy blanket that wraps around me and as I succumb to the weariness, a single thought lingers in my mind – how many more beginnings will I have to endure before I find my way home?

The initial warmth of John and Linda's home gradually cools into indifference. Days turn into a week, and the sense of being an outsider, a temporary fixture in their lives, grows stronger. The conversations at the dinner table became more about them and less inclusive of me. I can sense their interest in me waning, the strain of trying to incorporate a stranger into their lives becoming evident.

"Sarah, could you pass the salt?" Linda asks one evening, her voice lacking the warmth it once had.

"Sure," I reply, sliding the saltshaker across the table, my presence at the table feeling more like an obligation than a welcome.

As I lie in my bed that night, the feeling of being unwanted gnaws at me. It's a familiar ache, one that I've felt in countless other homes. The promise of stability and understanding, so often spoken, begins to feel like empty words, a script recited by every new set of foster parents I meet.

And then, just like that, I'm moving again. A social worker comes, a brief explanation given about a 'better fit' and 'temporary arrangement.' I pack my few belongings, the ritual feeling more automatic with each repetition.

The next home is different in appearance but similar in experience. The foster parents are polite, but their smiles don't reach their eyes. My room feels like a guest room, impersonal and temporary. My stay there lasts only a few days before I'm moved again.

In each new home, my presence feels more like a burden than a blessing. Conversations are brief and functional. "Dinner's at six," one foster mother tells me, her tone indicating that it's more of an announcement than an invitation.

I retreat further into myself, my responses becoming more mechanical. "Okay, thank you," I say, my words lacking any real emotion.

The cycle continues, each new home blending into the next in a blur of indifference and unfulfilled promises. With each move, the hope of finding a place where I belong fades, replaced by a deepening sense of isolation.

"Why do you keep moving me?" I finally ask my social worker during one of the transfers. My voice is tired, the question that I've pondered too often in silence.

"It's just... complicated, Sarah. We're trying to find the right fit for you," she replies, her tone sympathetic yet helpless.

But her words offer no comfort. They feel like another reminder of my transient existence, of my inability to find a place where I fit.

Mrs. Henderson's car pulls up to yet another foster home as the sun begins to set. Her words are a quiet prelude to what's become a familiar routine. "Sarah, this is just for a night or two. We're still looking for the right fit for you," she says, her voice a mix of apology and resignation.

I nod, the motion mechanical, devoid of any real expectation. I've heard similar assurances before, and they've become hollow, echoing in the void of my constant transitions.

The new foster home is a modest, unassuming house. Mrs. Henderson walks me to the door, and a woman opens it almost immediately. "Hi, I'm Mrs. Baker," she says, her smile warm but fleeting. "We're happy to have you, even if it's just for a short while."

"Thank you," I mutter, stepping inside. The house has a lived-in feel, but it's clear that no preparations were made for a new addition. I'm an unexpected guest, a fact that doesn't escape me.

Mrs. Baker shows me to a small room with a bed and a nightstand. "It's not much, but I hope you'll be comfortable here," she says before leaving me to settle in.

Alone in the room, I sit on the bed, feeling the weight of my bag in my lap. The room is plain, with none of the personal touches that would make it feel like a home. I'm just passing through, a transient shadow in the lives of these people.

As I lie down, the events of the past few days, the past few years, swirl in my mind. I think of my mother, her face a fading memory, but still a source of comfort. I remember Lily, Henry, and John, my siblings, now just distant echoes in my life. The pain of separation from them, from a life that once was, fills me, overwhelming in its intensity.

Tears start to stream down my face, each one a testament to the losses I've endured. I cry for my mother, for my siblings, for Michael, and for myself – a girl lost in a system that shuffles her from place to place, a system that has yet to find a place for her to truly call home.

I cry until exhaustion takes over, my sobs eventually giving way to a fitful sleep and the darkness of the night offers no solace. In the quiet of my temporary room, nightmares invade my sleep, each one more vivid and terrifying than the last. I see Michael, his face etched with the pain and despair that led to his tragic end. His eyes, once filled with warmth and laughter, now mirror the agony I feel every day.

I toss and turn, the sheets tangling around me as the scenes play out in my mind. The loss of Michael, the unspoken words, the shared dreams that crumbled with his passing – they haunt me, a relentless reminder of the love and life I lost.

But even more disturbing was the reoccurring nightmare of my stepfather, the man who inflicted so much pain and fear. I see the house with the red door, the very sight of it sending shivers down my spine. In my dreams, I'm back there, trapped, helpless, his menacing presence looming over me.

I wake up gasping for air, my heart racing, my body drenched in sweat. The room feels constricting, the walls closing in on me as the remnants of the nightmares linger. I lie there, trying to calm my racing heart, but the fear lingers, something I have grown accustomed to in the lonely hours of the night.

I sat up in bed, crying until my eyes burned and my head throbbed as I awaited Mrs. Henderson's return to bring me to my next "home".

I heard the knock on the door just after eight and

wasted no time as I grabbed the trash bag full of my belongings and ran to her car, not stopping to offer a goodbye. The next foster home was supposed to be another beginning, but as we approached, my heart dropped. The house, an ordinary structure in all respects, has one defining feature – a bright red front door. The color strikes a chord of terror in me, a visceral reminder of the abuse I suffered.

As the car comes to a stop, my breathing becomes rapid, shallow. Flashbacks flood my mind, each memory a sharp stab of fear. I can't do this, I can't face that door – it represents everything I've been trying to escape.

Without a word, I open the car door and start running. My only thought is to get as far away from that red door as possible. My heart pounds in my chest, each beat a frantic drum urging me to keep running, to escape the memories that door conjures.

The streets become a blur as I run, my mind reeling from the shock and fear. The freedom I thought I'd find in escaping is quickly overshadowed by a sense of vulnerability, of being utterly alone.

I stick to the shadows, avoiding the main streets, moving through alleys and side roads. Every sound makes me jump, every shadow a potential threat. I'm running from my past, but with each step, I feel it clinging to me, a relentless pursuer that I can't seem to shake off.

The city at night is a different world, one that feels more dangerous and unforgiving. I'm a lone figure, lost and scared, trying to navigate through a maze of uncertainty and fear. The feeling of being exposed, of being hunted, is overwhelming.

As the night wears on, the realization of my situation begins to sink in. I'm on the streets, with nowhere to go, running from demons that are as much in my mind as they are in the world. The sense of desperation grows, a gnawing fear that I've traded one form of captivity for another.

I stopped running, my lungs burning and my feet numb as I huddled in an alley, the cold of the night seeping into my bones. I'm out of breath, out of strength, and seemingly out of options. The stark reality of my situation sets in – I'm more lost than ever, caught in a never-ending cycle of fear and flight, searching for a safe haven that seems forever out of reach.

Without even realizing what was happening, I got up and walked to a bridge across the street when the wail of police sirens cut through the night, jolting me from my daze. I look up to see two officers approaching, their expressions a mix of concern and caution. I'm standing on the edge of the bridge, the dark waters below a silent witness to my turmoil.

"Sarah, please step away from the edge," one of the officers says, his voice steady but gentle.

I can feel the panic rising within me, a tide of fear and desperation. "I can't go back there. I can't," I say, my voice trembling, each word infused with a lifetime of pain and fear.

"We're not going to hurt you. We just want to help," the other officer assures me, taking a slow, non-threatening step closer.

But their words feel empty, hollow in the face of what I've experienced. "If you try to take me back, I'll jump," I say, the words spilling out in a rush. I don't know if I mean them, but the fear is real, the fear of returning to a place that represents everything I want to escape.

The officers exchange a look, their training kicking in. They back off slightly, their hands raised in a gesture of peace. "Okay, we're not going to force you. Let's just talk," the first officer says, his tone soothing.

"Why bother? You can't help me," I responded, my voice laced with skepticism.

"We're not here to force you into anything. We just want to understand," the second officer added, his tone gentle. "Tell us what's going on."

I hesitated, the turmoil inside me swirling. "It's like being trapped in a nightmare," I finally said, the words spilling out.

"We want to help you find a way out of that nightmare," the first officer replied, his voice sincere. "But you need to step back from the edge first."

Their words, simple yet earnest, slowly penetrated my wall of despair. After a moment, I took a reluctant step back, seeing the immediate relief in their expressions. However, my own eyes were clouded with fear of the unknown future that awaited me.

The journey back to the state hospital is a blur. I'm escorted in the back of the police car, the familiar sights passing by like specters in the night. Each mile brings a growing sense of defeat, a sinking realization that I'm returning to a cycle I've been trying to break free from.

As the hospital looms into view, a sense of despair washes over me. The building, with its imposing walls and dark windows, feels more like a prison than a haven. I'm led inside, the doors closing behind me with a finality that echoes in my heart.

Back in the sterile seclusion room that's become too familiar, I sit on the thin mattress, my gaze empty, my mind numb. The walls are bare, the space devoid of warmth or comfort. It's a stark reminder of my reality – a life caught between the fleeting hope of belonging and the crushing weight of rejection.

The sense of being adrift, of being perpetually unwanted and unloved, is overwhelming. The hospital, once a place I dreaded, has become a refuge of sorts, a twisted sanctuary from a world that seems to have no place for me. Here, at least, the expectations are clear, the disappointments predictable.

I lie on the mattress, staring at the ceiling. The faint hum of the hospital lights is a cold lullaby, lulling me into a restless sleep. In this place, I find a strange comfort in the familiarity of its walls, a bitter acceptance of its confines. It's a sanctuary, yes, but one that comes with its own set of chains – chains that bind me to a life of unending transitions and unfulfilled yearnings.

18 A BLEAK REALITY

Consciousness tiptoed back to me in fragments, like reluctant shadows fleeing from the relentless sun. My eyes flickered open, absorbing the barren whiteness of the room—a stark, unyielding expanse that pressed against my senses. The air tasted sterile and artificial. I was lying on a thin, narrow mattress on the floor, plastic with no sheets so my every move echoed through the room.

I tried to sit up, but a wave of dizziness forced me back down. My mind was a muddled mess, struggling to piece together the how's and why's of my arrival in this clinical seclusion.

A knock at the door shattered the eerie silence. The door opened with mechanical precision, and a staff member, Ms. Brown, stepped in. She was a stern figure, her face etched with lines of disapproval and weariness. "Sarah," she began, her voice lacking any warmth, "you are to remain here, in seclusion."

"Why?" My voice sounded weak, even to my own ears.

"Your behavior has been... troubling. We don't want you influencing the younger patients negatively. This is for your own good as much as theirs."

I wanted to protest, to scream that I wasn't some malevolent force corrupting innocent minds. But the words lodged in my throat, unspoken.

The room felt like a tangible manifestation of my inner turmoil. Its small size and the absence of windows created a claustrophobic atmosphere that seemed to echo my own feelings of entrapment. The walls, a clinical white, were bare and unyielding, offering no comfort or distraction from my spiraling thoughts. A staff member sat in the doorway but paid me no mind.

Hours dragged by, each second stretching into an eternity. I lay there, my thoughts a chaotic whirlpool. Memories surfaced, unbidden. I remembered the laughter of the other patients, the brief moments of camaraderie that had been a balm to my fractured spirit. Now, even those fleeting connections were severed.

I thought about my life, and how it had spiraled out

of control. Seventeen years old now, and what did I have to show for it? A string of broken friendships, a trail of disappointment, and now, confinement in a room that felt more like a tomb than a place of healing.

The seclusion was more than physical; it was a mirror to my own isolation, the chasm that had widened between me and the rest of the world. I was an island, cut off from the mainland of normalcy and understanding. I wondered if anyone out there thought of me, if anyone missed the girl I used to be before the world turned cold and unfeeling.

Time lost its meaning in the seclusion room. Days melded into nights, indistinguishable but for the shift in light that seeped through the cracks beneath the door. The world outside continued its relentless march, oblivious to the stagnation of my existence.

The regular administration of Haldol and Thorazine became the only landmarks in the barren landscape of my days. Each dose was delivered with clinical detachment by nurses whose faces blurred into one another, their expressions masked by professional neutrality.

"Time for your medication, Sarah," they would say, their voices devoid of any inflection. The pills lay in my palm like small, potent symbols of surrender. I resisted at first, stubbornly clinging to the sharp edges of my pain, afraid that to let go would be to lose myself entirely. But resistance waned under the relentless tide of despair.

The sedatives wove their way through my system, a chemical embrace that dulled the sharpness of my thoughts. They brought a numbness that was almost welcome in their ability to smother the relentless anguish that gnawed at my soul. My mind drifted in a foggy haze, untethered from the harsh realities that had driven me to this point.

I became a spectator to my own life, observing the slow, rhythmic passage of time with a detachment that bordered on the surreal. The side effects of the medication manifested themselves subtly at first, drowsiness that blurred the lines between waking and sleeping, and disorientation that made the room spin in slow, lazy circles.

But as the weeks turned into months, the effects deepened. My thoughts grew sluggish, struggling to wade through the mental mire. My body felt heavy, as if weighed down by an invisible force. The world seemed distant, a play enacted on a stage far removed from my own reality.

Sometimes, in moments of lucid despair, I would

try to remember who I was before the sedation, and before the seclusion. Fragments of memories floated to the surface—laughter, sunlight, a sense of belonging—but they slipped away, elusive and intangible.

I lay on the bed, staring at the ceiling, the white expanse a blank canvas for my dulled thoughts. The staff member who was always at my door was a silent witness to my slow unraveling.

In this chemically induced limbo, I found a perverse comfort. The drugs shielded me from the full force of my emotions, from the memories that lurked in the dark corners of my mind. But they also stole something essential, leaving behind a shell where a person used to be.

The nurses came and went, their visits a monotonous routine that punctuated the endless days. Their words washed over me, their voices distant echoes that barely registered in my sedated consciousness.

"Sarah, how are you feeling today?" they would ask, a question that seemed absurd in its simplicity.

"I'm fine," I would reply, the words automatic and devoid of meaning. Fine was a concept that no longer applied to me, a state of being that belonged to a different life, a different Sarah.

As I drifted in and out of sleep, the line between reality and dreams blurred. Time continued its inexorable march, indifferent to the girl trapped in a white-walled purgatory, lost in a sea of medication and despair.

As the time in seclusion stretched into a monotonous tapestry, my initial resistance to the sedatives began to wane, replaced by a reluctant acceptance. The numbing blanket they cast over my mind offered a respite, however fleeting, from the gnawing sense of being unloved and unwanted. In the depths of my drug-induced sleep, I found solace, a temporary haven from the relentless turmoil of my waking hours.

It was during one of these listless afternoons that a visit from the hospital social worker heralded a significant change. The staff member at the door stepped aside and Ms. Dixon entered, her usual stern expression tinged with an unfamiliar solemnity.

"Sarah, there's something we need to discuss," she began, her voice carrying a weight that immediately set my nerves on edge.

I sat up, a sense of foreboding tightening in my chest. "What is it?"

"You're being transferred to the adult ward," she announced, her words slicing through the room's stagnant air.

The news struck me like a physical blow. The adult ward? The very idea filled me with a deep, visceral fear. I'd heard whispers about it - a place where the more unstable, older patients were housed. The thought of being among them, of leaving the familiar albeit oppressive confines of this room, was daunting.

"But why?" My voice was a mere whisper, choked by the rising tide of anxiety.

"It's what was decided. You're seventeen now, Sarah. With your past behavior, you are no longer a good fit for the adolescent ward."

Her explanation did little to quell the panic that clawed at my insides. I felt like a small boat being swept away into an unforgiving sea, unprepared and vulnerable.

The day of the transfer arrived with a suffocating inevitability. Two unfamiliar staff members came to escort me, their faces masks of professional detachment. As we walked through the corridors, the reality of my situation set in. I was leaving behind the known for the unknown, stepping into a world that seemed far more intimidating.

The adult ward was a stark contrast to the juvenile wing. The atmosphere was heavier, charged with an undercurrent of unpredictability. The patients I passed seemed more weathered by life, their eyes reflecting stories of hardships I could only imagine.

My new room was similar to the rooms on the adolescence ward but felt colder, and more impersonal. The walls were the same sterile white, but they loomed larger as if holding back a sea of untold stories. The mattress was replaced by a bed, I was given sheets to put on it, and I had a bigger window but it was obstructed by a giant bush.

The staff here were less familiar, their interactions with me more clinical and distant. I missed the occasional gentleness of the staff from the adolescent ward, even though it had been sparse.

As I sat on the bed, a sense of isolation wrapped itself around me like a shroud. I was in a new world, one that seemed far more daunting and unpredictable than anything I had faced before.

The first night in the adult ward was the longest of

my life. Sounds of distress and confusion echoed down the hallways, a constant reminder of where I was. I lay on the bed, staring at the ceiling, feeling the weight of countless eyes upon me, eyes that had seen more of life's darkness than I had.

Fear became my constant partner, whispering tales of despair in the long, sleepless hours of the night. I clung to the sedatives like a lifeline, the only thing keeping me adrift in this new sea of uncertainty.

As dawn broke, casting a weak light into my room, I realized that this transfer marked the end of one chapter of my life and the beginning of another, far more uncertain one. I was no longer a child in the eyes of the world, but what I had become in its stead was a mystery, even to myself.

In the adult ward, my sense of isolation was paradoxically amplified by the constant presence of another. Assigned more 1:1 supervision due to my age, I found myself under the relentless watch of a staff member. This unceasing vigilance stripped away the last vestiges of my privacy, making every moment feel like an intrusion.

The staff member assigned to me, a woman named Ms. Carter, followed me like a shadow. Her presence was a constant reminder of my vulnerability, a tangible manifestation of the control the institution had over me.

"I'm just here to ensure your safety," Ms. Carter would say in a tone that suggested this was a well-rehearsed line. Her eyes, though not unkind, held a professional detachment that made any attempt at connection feel futile.

My days became a monotonous cycle of meals, medication, and therapy sessions, all under the watchful eye of my 1:1. The lack of privacy felt suffocating, each moment observed and noted. I longed for a moment of solitude, a chance to breathe without feeling the weight of another's gaze upon me.

As I adjusted to this new normal, my inner world became a tumultuous sea of thoughts and fears. I felt more vulnerable than ever, a small boat adrift in a vast and uncaring ocean. The absence of real human connection left a gaping void in my soul, one that seemed to grow with each passing day.

In therapy sessions, I would sit across from the therapist, my words feeling hollow and rehearsed. "I'm coping," I would say, a lie that tasted bitter on my tongue. My assigned staff member sat nearby, a silent observer to these exchanges.

"How are you adjusting to the adult ward?" the therapist would ask, her pen poised above her notebook.

"It's... different," I would reply, my voice barely a whisper. Different was a vast understatement. It was a world apart, a stark landscape where hope seemed a distant memory.

The nights were the hardest. Lying in bed, the faint sounds of the ward around me, I felt the crushing weight of my reality. The darkness seemed to press in from all sides, a physical entity that fed on my fear and despair.

In those long hours, my mind would wander to the life I had left behind. Memories of laughter, like the time my mother took my siblings and I down to the park with all the neighbor kids and we played kick ball until well after dark. The memories of warmth and of a time when the world hadn't seemed so bleak, would surface, teasing me with their unattainability. Tears would often come, silent and unnoticed, soaking into my pillow.

The interaction with other patients was minimal and always under the watchful eye of the staff. Their stories, their pain, echoed my own, yet the chasm between us remained vast and unbridgeable.

"I miss the stars," I once confided to Ms. Carter during a rare moment of vulnerability.

She had looked at me, a flicker of something akin to sympathy in her eyes. "I understand," she had said, but the words felt empty, unable to bridge the gap between us.

As days turned into weeks, I settled into a routine that felt like a dance with despair. Each step was measured, each movement a mimicry of living. I was going through the motions, a ghost haunting the corridors of a life that no longer felt like my own.

In this new world of constant supervision and enforced routine, I felt like a specimen under a microscope, observed and analyzed but never truly seen. The sense of being a perpetual outsider, of being fundamentally different, grew with each passing day. The adult ward, with its rules and restrictions, its clinical detachment, was a universe away from any semblance of the life I had once dreamed of.

19 A SECRET FLAME

The unyielding rhythm of life in the adult ward had worn me down, each day chipping away at the remnants of my spirit. The constant presence of supervision, the ceaseless hum of activity—it all became an oppressive cloak I couldn't shake off. More than anything, I craved a moment of solitude, a brief respite from the ever-watchful eyes that seemed to follow my every move.

One evening, as the ward settled into its nocturnal routine, a restless energy took hold of me. The staff member who was assigned as my 1:1 for the shift sat in his usual spot, his eyes periodically glancing up from his phone to ensure I was still within sight. I felt a desperate need to escape, even if just for a few moments.

With a quiet, almost stealthy movement, I slid off my bed and crawled under my desk. It was a small space, cramped and dusty, but to me, it was a haven.

The desk's wood was cool against my skin, the shadows a comforting embrace compared to the harsh fluorescent lights of the ward.

Underneath that desk, I allowed myself a luxury I hadn't indulged in for what seemed like an eternity. I cried. My sobs were muffled by the thick silence of the room, my tears soaking into the sweatshirt I was issued upon arrival.

Here, in this tiny sanctuary, I was shielded from the prying eyes of the world. I was alone with my thoughts, a luxury that had become increasingly rare. The weight of constant surveillance, the burden of being perpetually watched—it all melted away in the shadows under the desk.

In that confined space, I confronted the raw essence of my loneliness. It was a palpable thing, a heavy presence that sat on my chest, making it hard to breathe. I thought of the outside world, of people living lives untouched by the stifling walls of institutions like this. A pang of sorrow for the life I was missing out on, a life of freedom and choices, gripped me.

The fear that had become a constant in my life also crept in, whispering doubts and insecurities. I was afraid of the future, of the unknown paths that lay ahead. I was afraid of being forgotten, a mere footnote in the lives of those who had once known me.

Under that desk, in the quiet of my self-made solitude, I allowed myself to feel it all—the loneliness, the sorrow, the fear. It was overwhelming, a tidal wave that threatened to consume me, but it was also a release, a momentary liberation from the facade I maintained for the world outside.

"I miss being seen," I whispered to the darkness, my voice choked with tears. "I miss being Sarah."

Huddled beneath the desk, my heart pounded against my ribcage, a staccato rhythm that mirrored my chaotic thoughts. The dim light cast long shadows across the room, creating an illusion of seclusion. It was in this fragile sanctuary that an unexpected discovery shattered my illusion of solitude.

Footsteps approached, haltingly at first, then with a determined cadence. I held my breath, bracing myself for confrontation. The footsteps ceased near my desk, and in the dim light, a pair of eyes locked onto mine. They belonged to Derik, the male employee assigned to monitor me. Not much taller than me, his athletic build was noticeable even in the shadowy room. His dark hair, always styled with precision, contrasted sharply with his chiseled jawline, adding to his intimidating presence.

"Sarah?" His voice was a low whisper, tinged with curiosity rather than anger.

I remained silent, frozen in place, my mind racing with the possible consequences of being found.

To my astonishment, he grabbed my arm and pulled me out from under the desk, his movements careful and deliberate. The contact was unexpected, his touch startlingly gentle. He helped me stand, and in a moment that felt suspended in time, he kissed me.

The kiss was soft, and hesitant, and it jolted me with a mixture of shock and terror. It was a kind of touch I hadn't experienced in a long while—a human connection so starkly absent in my life within these walls. My initial reaction was to pull away, but a part of me was starved for affection, desperate for a semblance of normalcy in the abnormality of my existence.

He stepped back, his eyes searching mine. "I'm sorry, I shouldn't have..." he murmured, his voice laden with a mix of regret and something else I couldn't quite place.

In the quiet of the room, he whispered, " I love you,

Sarah." The words hung in the air, heavy and disorienting. I stood there, grappling with a maelstrom of emotions. There was an inherent inappropriateness in his declaration, a boundary crossed that shouldn't have been. Yet, there was a part of me, long suppressed and buried, that clung to his words like a lifeline.

"I... I don't know what to say," I stammered, my voice barely above a whisper.

"You don't have to say anything," he replied, his expression one of vulnerability. "I just wanted you to know. I have loved you since the moment I saw you in restraints on the adolescent ward."

The complexity of the situation was overwhelming. He was an employee, an adult who should have been helping to guide me, offering a connection that was as forbidden as it was desperately craved. It was a connection that transcended the sterile, impersonal interactions I had grown accustomed to.

We stood there, two souls adrift in the sea of our circumstances, finding an unexpected anchor in each other's presence. The moment was fleeting, yet it left an indelible mark on my heart.

As he walked away, leaving me to process the myriad emotions coursing through me, I realized how profoundly starved I was for love, for a connection that went beyond the superficial. His confession, though startling, had awakened something within me—a longing for understanding, for acceptance, for a bond that resonated with the very core of my being.

In the solitude that followed, I contemplated the complexity of human emotions, the tangled web of needs and desires that defined our existence. His words echoed in my mind, a haunting reminder of the profound need for connection that lies at the heart of us all.

"Are you okay, Sarah?" Ms. Carter asked, her voice tinged with something that might have been a genuine concern.

I nodded, not trusting myself to speak. I climbed back onto my bed, feeling the weight of her gaze on me once more as her and Derik traded spots. But something had shifted inside me. In the silence and solitude under that desk, I had touched a part of myself I thought I had lost. It was a small victory, but in the confines of the adult ward, it felt significant.

As I lay there, staring at the ceiling, I realized that

no matter how much they watched me, no matter how much they tried to control my environment, there were parts of me they could never reach. In my mind, in my heart, I was still Sarah, and that was something no amount of surveillance could take away.

The clandestine nature of my meetings with Derik cast a veil of excitement over my otherwise monotonous days. We would steal moments together, our interactions imbued with a tenderness that contrasted sharply with the stark, clinical environment of the ward. Yet, beneath the surface of this budding romance, there was an undeniable tension—a constant awareness of the forbidden and risky nature of our relationship.

Each secret encounter with Derik was like a breath of fresh air in the suffocating atmosphere of the hospital. His presence brought a semblance of normalcy, a reminder of a world beyond these walls. In his eyes, I saw a reflection of myself not as a patient, but as Sarah, a person with hopes, fears, and desires.

Our conversations were whispers in the shadows, our touches fleeting yet charged with meaning. In these moments, I found a happiness I thought had been irrevocably lost. Derik's smile, his laughter, the way he looked at me—all of it offered a temporary escape from the grim reality of my life.

But amidst this newfound joy, there was a persistent undercurrent of guilt and confusion. I was acutely aware of the moral ambiguity of our relationship. The thrill of the secret, the exhilaration of defying the rules, was tinged with the knowledge that what we were doing was fraught with ethical complexities.

"Are we doing something wrong?" I once asked Derik during one of our covert meetings.

He paused, his expression one of contemplation. "It feels right when I'm with you, Sarah. But I know it's... complicated."

The word 'complicated' resonated with me. Our relationship existed in a gray area, where the rules of the outside world seemed distorted. The power dynamics, the setting of our encounters, the reality of our individual circumstances—all of it contributed to a landscape where right and wrong were not easily discernable.

Despite these complexities, I couldn't deny the profound connection I felt with Derik. He saw me for who I was, beyond the diagnosis and the treatments. With him, I could be vulnerable, I could be myself.

Yet, in the quiet moments alone, I wrestled with my conscience. Was our relationship a genuine connection, or was it a product of manipulation, a response to the deprivation of affection and normalcy? The thrill of our secret meetings was constantly overshadowed by the fear of discovery and the potential consequences it would bring.

As our relationship deepened, so did the intensity of my emotions. Happiness, guilt, excitement, and fear melded into a complex tapestry that colored my every thought. Derik had become a beacon of light in the darkness of my world, but with every stolen moment, I couldn't shake the feeling that we were walking a precarious tightrope, one that could snap at any moment.

In the depth of my heart, I knew that our forbidden romance was a double-edged sword—a source of joy as much as a potential catalyst for further pain. The complexity of my emotions mirrored the complexity of our situation, each day weaving a more intricate web of feelings and moral dilemmas.

One evening before bed, I found myself at a crossroads, caught between the exhilaration of this secret romance and the sobering reality of our circumstances. The path ahead was shrouded in uncertainty, each step forward a venture into uncharted territory. It was during this stolen moment, in the dim light of the evening, that Derik shared the news that set my heart racing with both excitement and trepidation.

"I found out something incredible, Sarah," he whispered, his eyes shining with a mixture of joy and fear. "You're being moved to a new foster home. It's near where I live."

The news hit me like a wave, leaving me momentarily breathless. A new foster home—a change in environment, a step into the unknown. But it was his next words that truly sent my mind spinning.

"I want to pick you up there. We can go on a real date, Sarah. Just you and me, outside these walls."

The thought of being with Derik, free from the constraints of the hospital, was exhilarating. A real date, something so normal and yet so out of reach for so long, felt like a dream. But it was a dream laced with danger, the peril of our situation hanging over us like a dark cloud.

"We have to be careful," I murmured, the weight of the risk we were taking pressing down on me.

"I know," he replied, his hand squeezing mine. "But it's worth it, for you."

That night, as I lay in my bed, the reality of the recent turn of events slowly sank in. The dim light of the room cast long shadows, mirroring the play of emotions within me. Joy and fear intertwined, each vying for dominance.

I was about to embark on a new chapter of my life, both literally and figuratively. The prospect of leaving the hospital, of stepping into a new home, was daunting yet filled with potential. And then there was Derik—his presence in my life had become something I cherished, a signal of hope in a world that had often felt devoid of it.

But with this hope came the fear of the consequences. Our relationship, hidden in the shadows of the hospital, was a delicate secret, one that could unravel with the slightest misstep. The thought of being discovered, of the repercussions that could follow, sent a shiver down my spine.

As I drifted into a restless sleep, my mind was a tangle of thoughts and emotions. The excitement of being with Derik, of experiencing a sliver of normalcy, was intoxicating. Yet, the fear of what lay ahead, the potential for everything to come crashing down, was a specter that loomed large in the darkness.

20 THE BREAKING POINT

The moment I stepped into my new foster home, a wave of warmth enveloped me, washing away the sterile coldness of the hospital. The house was a picture of suburban bliss, nestled in a quiet neighborhood with a neatly manicured lawn. A young couple, Mr. and Mrs. Johnson, stood at the door, their smiles genuine and welcoming. Beside them were their two young sons, their curious eyes peeking at me shyly.

"Welcome, Sarah. We're so glad to have you with us," Mrs. Johnson said, her voice soft and inviting.

"Thank you," I replied, my voice barely above a whisper, overwhelmed by the sudden shift from isolation to familial warmth.

The house was alive with the sounds of a family – the distant laughter of the boys playing, the comforting hum of the kitchen appliances, the gentle creak of the wooden floors. Mr. Johnson led me to my room, a cozy space painted in soft pastels, with a large window that framed a view of a serene garden. The room felt like a sanctuary, a personal haven that was worlds away from the sterile, confined space I had grown accustomed to.

Over the next few days, I found myself slowly melding into the rhythm of the household. I helped with chores, the simplicity of the tasks bringing an unexpected sense of satisfaction. Washing dishes, folding laundry, and preparing meals became meditative activities, grounding me in the present moment.

Dinners were a new experience – a time for sharing and laughter. The family gathered around the table, exchanging stories of their day. I listened, mostly quiet, but the sound of their voices, the easy banter, filled me with a sense of belonging. I was part of something, no longer an observer from the sidelines.

"Sarah, how was school today?" Mrs. Johnson would ask, her interest sincere.

"It was good," I'd respond, still getting used to the idea of attending school again. The classroom was a microcosm of the world I had been removed from, a world I was now cautiously re-entering.

The boys, curious and energetic, slowly warmed up to me. "Do you want to play a game with us after dinner?" the younger one, Tommy, asked one evening, his eyes bright with hope.

"I'd like that," I said, smiling genuinely for the first time in what felt like ages.

Playing board games with them, I felt a rush of normalcy, a return to a life I thought I had lost. I was no longer just a patient or a case file – I was Sarah, a sister, a family member, a friend.

Each night, as I lay in my new bed, the moonlight casting gentle shadows across my room, I reflected on the day. The joy of simple things – a shared meal, a laughter-filled game, a conversation about mundane daily happenings – filled me with a sense of contentment I hadn't felt in years.

For the first time in a long time, I allowed myself to believe in the possibility of a better future, one where I could be more than my past, more than my struggles. In this house, with this family, I was starting to feel like a regular teenager, experiencing a life that was both wonderfully ordinary and profoundly new.

Despite the newfound comfort of my foster home, my mind was often elsewhere, consumed by thoughts of Derik. Our secret plans to meet were a thrilling escape from the routine, a rebellion against the confines of my new, structured life. I knew it was risky, but the thought of seeing him, of being with him without the walls of the hospital around us, was intoxicating.

Lying in bed one evening, my heart pounded against my chest with anticipation. The clock's hands seemed to move agonizingly slow as I waited for 8 pm. I had planned everything meticulously – I knew the family's routines, the quietest ways to exit the house, the exact spot where Derik and I would meet. It was a few streets away, far enough to avoid being seen but close enough to feel safe.

 My plan, however, came undone just as it was about to begin. As I cautiously opened my bedroom door, the faint creak of the hinges betraying my intentions, I was startled by a voice.

"Sarah, where are you going?" It was my foster mother, her figure emerging from the shadows of the hallway. Her voice was laced with concern, but there was an underlying firmness to it.

"I was just... going for a walk. I couldn't sleep," I stammered, the lie feeling clumsy on my tongue.

"At this hour?" She crossed her arms, her expression turning from concern to suspicion. "It's late, and it's not safe."

The tension in the air thickened, a tangible force between us. I could see the worry in her eyes, the fear that perhaps she didn't know me as well as she thought.

"I'm sorry, I just... I needed some air," I replied, my voice barely above a whisper. The thrill of rebellion had been replaced by a sinking feeling of guilt.

"We care about you, Sarah. We just want you to be safe," she said, her voice softening. "Is there something you're not telling us?"

The question hung in the air, heavy with implication. The pressure of keeping my relationship with Derik a secret, coupled with the effort of adapting to this new life, was overwhelming. I felt cornered, caught between my desire for freedom and the reality of my situation.

"I'm sorry," I repeated, the words inadequate for the turmoil I felt inside. Tears began to well up in my eyes, the emotional dam breaking.

She stepped forward, her demeanor shifting from authority to empathy. "Sarah, whatever it is, you can talk to us. We're here to help you, not to judge."

"Why can't I just have this one thing for myself?" I blurted out, my voice trembling with a mix of defiance and desperation. "Why does everyone always have to control everything I do?"

My foster mother's expression softened, but her concern was evident. "Sarah, we're not trying to control you. We're worried about you. It's late, and it's not safe for you to be out alone."

Her words, meant to be reassuring, only fueled my frustration. "I'm not a child," I snapped, the need to assert my independence overpowering my better judgment. "I can make my own decisions."

She sighed, a deep, weary exhalation. "I know you're not a child, but you're still under our care. We're responsible for you, and we can't just let you wander off in the middle of the night."

Her logical arguments were lost on me, drowned out by the roaring in my ears, the overwhelming desire to break free from all the rules and restrictions.

"I'm tired of always being told what to do, of always being watched. I just wanted one night, one moment to feel normal," I said, my voice breaking.

There was a long, heavy silence between us. I could see the conflict in her eyes, the struggle to find the right balance between care and control.

The argument with my foster mother escalated quickly, the air between us charged with anger and frustration. Her words, though spoken with concern, felt like shackles, tightening around me, suffocating the last bit of freedom I thought I had.

"Why can't you just trust me?" I shouted, my voice raw with emotion. "Why does everyone always assume they know what's best for me?"

"Sarah, it's not about trust. It's about safety, about making sure you're okay," she replied, her voice strained, trying to bridge the gap of understanding between us.

But her words only ignited further rebellion within me. "You don't understand. Nobody does! I'm not just some problem you can fix with rules and curfews. I have feelings, I have a life outside of this house!"

The intensity of my own words surprised me, a torrent of long-suppressed emotions pouring out. My foster mother's face registered shock, then hurt, as she absorbed the full force of my outburst.

"Sarah, I'm only trying to help you. But you need to be honest with us. Are you meeting someone? Is that why you wanted to go out?" she asked, her voice a mix of concern and accusation.

The question hit me like a slap. The truth about Derik, our secret relationship, hung in the air, unspoken but palpable. I faltered, the facade crumbling under her piercing gaze.

"Yes, I was meeting someone," I admitted, my voice barely above a whisper. "But it's not what you think. He's the only one who understands me, who sees me for who I am."

Her reaction was immediate, a mix of betrayal and concern. "Sarah, you're putting yourself in danger. We can't allow that. We need to know who this person is."

The conversation spiraled from there, my protests clashing against her insistence on knowing more about Derik. Each word we exchanged widened the rift between us, my longing for understanding battling against her need to protect.

In the aftermath of our heated exchange, I felt a sense of desolation. My room, once a haven, now felt like a familiar prison. I lay on my bed, staring at the ceiling, engulfed by a sense of helplessness. The internal chaos I felt was mirrored in my actions, a self-destructive spiral that seemed impossible to escape.

My foster mother, driven by her concern for my well-being, began to unravel the layers of secrecy surrounding my relationship with Derik. Feeling a mix of betrayal and fear for my safety, she made the difficult decision to report the situation. Her actions, though meant to protect me, felt like the ultimate breach of trust.

This decision set in motion a series of events that were both swift and unyielding. Within days, I found myself being uprooted once again, my brief taste of normalcy and happiness dissolving into thin air. I was being sent to a new home, away from the fragile connections I had begun to form.

As I packed my few belongings, a deep sense of anger and sadness engulfed me. I felt misunderstood, a pawn in a game where I had no control. The prospect of starting over yet again, of trying to fit into another new environment, was daunting. I was tired, tired of the constant upheaval, tired of fighting a battle that seemed to have no end.

The next morning as I sat in the back of Mrs. Henderson's car, being driven to my new home. My gaze was fixed on the passing scenery, but my mind was elsewhere, lost in a whirlwind of emotions. Anger, sadness, betrayal, and fear swirled within me, the familiar tumultuous storm that showed no signs of abating. As the car moved further away from what had briefly been my home, I was left to contemplate the uncertain road ahead, a path fraught with challenges and devoid of any clear direction.

The car ride to my new foster home was a blur, my thoughts racing. Upon arrival, I was greeted with polite, but distant smiles – another set of strangers in another strange home. Before I could even settle in, I was met with a devastating revelation.

Mrs. Henderson turned to me before walking back to her car. Her expression was somber as she sat down on the steps to speak with me. "Sarah, there's something you need to know," she began, her voice heavy with a seriousness that immediately set off alarms in my mind.

I braced myself, sensing the bad news. "What is it?" I asked, my voice barely audible.

"It's about Derik," she said, her eyes meeting mine with a look of genuine concern. "He no longer works at the hospital. There's an investigation... he's in trouble."

The words hit me like a physical blow. Derik, the

one person who had been my solace, my escape from the relentless challenges of my life, was now out of reach, entangled in troubles that seemed insurmountable.

"What kind of trouble?" I managed to ask, though a part of me wasn't sure I wanted to know.

"It's a serious matter, Sarah. He's under investigation for misconduct. I can't give you all the details, but it's best you don't contact him right now," she explained, her tone gentle yet firm.

I felt a wave of despair wash over me, the implications of her words slowly sinking in. Betrayal, loss, confusion – a chaotic mix of emotions churned within me. The one person I had trusted, who I believed understood me, was now another source of pain, another letdown in a life that seemed full of them.

The conversation with Ms. Henderson continued, her words a distant echo as I grappled with this new reality. She talked about my upcoming 18th birthday, the transition plans, including a small fund from the state to help me get started on my own, and the support systems in place, but it all felt meaningless, a bureaucratic process that seemed disconnected from the turmoil I was experiencing.

As she left, I sat alone in my new room, a space that felt both foreign and confining. The walls were bare, the window looking out to a world that felt increasingly alien. The threads of my life, which I had so desperately tried to hold together, had unraveled with alarming speed.

I lay on my bed, staring blankly at the ceiling, lost in the maze of my thoughts. The consequences of my actions weighed heavily on me – the loss of my last foster home, the possible severing of my connection with Derik, and the uncertainty of my future as I neared adulthood.

I felt a profound sense of isolation and betrayal. The people I had leaned on, the dreams I had cherished, all seemed to have slipped through my fingers like sand. I was left to contemplate the path ahead, a journey that was mine to navigate, fraught with challenges and devoid of any clear direction. As I lay there, the last rays of sunlight fading from my room, I realized that the approaching dawn of my 18th birthday brought with it not just a year older in age, but a stark awakening to the complexities and harsh realities of the world I was about to enter.

21 INCEPTION OF ADULTHOOD

The first light of dawn crept through the curtains of my room as I awoke on my 18th birthday. Lying in bed, I stared at the ceiling, feeling a peculiar blend of freedom and uncertainty. Today marked the official end of my childhood, a threshold into adulthood that I had both longed for and dreaded.

I sat up, taking a deep breath. Today was more than just a birthday; it was a symbol of independence, a liberation from the institutionalized environments and foster systems that had defined so much of my life. Yet, with this newfound freedom came a heavy weight of responsibility and the unknown.

As I got dressed, my thoughts drifted to the past – the endless cycle of foster homes, the sterile corridors of the hospital, the faces of caregivers who had come and gone. Each had left an imprint on me, shaping the person I had become.

The morning's routine was uneventful, yet there was

a palpable sense of change in the air. At breakfast, my foster mother, Mrs. Allen, gave me a small, sad smile. "Happy birthday, Sarah," she said, her voice carrying a tone of hollow sadness.

"Thank you, Mrs. Allen," I replied, managing a weak smile in return. The atmosphere at the table was subdued, the usual morning chatter replaced by a somber silence.

After breakfast, Mrs. Allen handed me a white trash bag. It contained the few belongings I had accumulated over my time in foster care – a couple of pairs of clothes, a book, and a few hygiene items. The simplicity of my possessions was a stark reminder of the transient nature of my life so far.

"Here are your things," she said, her eyes avoiding mine. "I hope you find what you're looking for out there."

The farewell was brief and impersonal, a far cry from the warm, tearful goodbyes I had seen in movies or read about in books. It was a stark reminder that this place was just another temporary stop in my journey – not a home, but a waypoint.

As I stood at the front door, the trash bag in hand, a sense of surrealism washed over me. This was it – the moment I stepped out of the structured world of childhood and into the vast, open landscape of adulthood.

The door closed behind me with a soft click, the sound echoing in my ears. I took a deep breath, feeling a mix of exhilaration and apprehension. The road ahead was uncharted, filled with possibilities and perils.

I turned to face the world outside, the morning sun casting long shadows on the pavement. Today, I was no longer a child in the eyes of the law. Today, I was an adult, free to make my own choices, and forge my own path.

But with that freedom came questions that loomed large in my mind. Where would I go? What would I do? Who would I become? The answers were unclear, hidden in the mists of the future.

As I walked down the driveway, the weight of the trash bag in my hand, I realized that this was more than just a physical journey. It was a journey of self-discovery, a quest to find my place in a world that had often felt unwelcoming and cold.

The chapter of childhood had closed, and the pages of adulthood lay open before me, blank and waiting to be filled. With a mixture of fear and hope, I stepped forward into the dawn of my new life.

I walked down the street, the weight of my past and the uncertainty of my future battled within me. It was then that I saw her - my mother, standing by a car parked at the curb, her eyes searching until they found mine. Beside her were my three siblings, their faces a mix of curiosity and excitement.

"Sarah!" my mother called out, her voice trembling with a cocktail of emotions. She approached me, her steps hesitant, as if she was afraid I might vanish.

"Hi, Mom," I replied, my voice steadier than I felt. Seeing her brought back a flood of memories – some warm, others painful.

"We've missed you so much," she said, her eyes welling up with tears. "We want you to come home, Sarah. We can be a family again."

Her words tugged at my heartstrings. I longed for the comfort of family, the sense of belonging that home promised. But something within me resisted – the desire for independence, for a life I could call my own.

"Mom, I love you all, and I miss you too," I began, choosing my words carefully. "But I need to do this on my own. I've found a place. I want to try living by myself."

The tension in the air was palpable. My siblings exchanged glances, unsure of how to react. My mother looked at me, a mixture of pride and concern in her eyes.

"Are you sure, Sarah? It's not going to be easy," she said, her maternal instincts on full display.

"I know, Mom. But I need to try. This is something I have to do for myself," I replied, my resolve firm.

There was a moment of silence, a mutual understanding passing between us. Then, slowly, my mother nodded. "Okay, Sarah. We'll support you. Just know that we're here for you, always."

The rest of the day was spent signing a lease and setting up my new home. It was a small and modest one, but to me, it was a castle – a symbol of my newfound freedom. My mother and siblings helped, moving in the few pieces of furniture we had gotten from a thrift store, and arranging things here and there.

As we worked, there was laughter and storytelling, moments of connection that we hadn't shared in a long time. My siblings were curious about my new life, their questions innocent yet poignant.

"Will you come to visit us, Sarah?" my youngest

sister asked, her eyes wide with hope.

"Of course, I will," I promised, ruffling her hair. "I'll visit often. We're still family, no matter where I live."

By evening, the house began to feel like a home. My family stayed for dinner, a simple meal we prepared together in my small kitchen. There was a sense of camaraderie, a rebuilding of bridges long left neglected.

As they left, my mother hugged me tightly. "I'm proud of you, Sarah. You're stronger than you know."

Standing at the doorway, watching them drive away, I felt a surge of mixed emotions. There was sadness in their departure, but also a sense of accomplishment. I had taken a step forward, one that led me away from the shadows of my past and into the light of a future I was beginning to shape.

I sat in my recliner in the quiet of my new home, a space that was entirely mine. I was alone, but not lonely, surrounded by the echoes of a family reconnecting and the promise of a life filled with possibilities. The challenges ahead were many, but for the first time, I felt ready to face them, armed with a sense of purpose and a newfound maturity.

The sun had just begun to dip below the horizon when Derik arrived. His knock on my door was hesitant, a stark contrast to the confident taps I had grown accustomed to. When I opened the door, I was greeted with a face that was familiar, yet strangely altered.

"Hey, Sarah," Derik greeted, his voice lacking its usual warmth. There was something in his eyes, a flicker of something unreadable, that sent a ripple of unease through me.

"Hi, Derik. Come in," I replied, stepping aside to let him enter. As he walked past me, I caught a whiff of his cologne, a scent that had once brought me comfort, now mingling with the unfamiliar smells of my new house.

We sat down, and I could feel the tension radiating off him. He kept glancing at his phone, his leg bouncing with nervous energy. "Are you okay?" I asked, concern lacing my words.

"Yeah, yeah, I'm fine. Just... a lot on my mind, you know?" he replied, forcing a smile that seemed fake.

I wanted to believe him, to brush off the nagging

feeling in my gut that something was amiss. But the Derik sitting before me was a shadow of the person I knew.

After a few moments of strained conversation, he stood up abruptly. "Listen, Sarah, I need to run out for a bit. I want to pick up some things for your new place."

"Okay, sure. Do you want me to come with you?" I offered, sensing an opportunity to understand what was troubling him.

"No, I want it to be a surprise, but I'll tell ya what. How about we drive over to my place and you can make yourself at home there while you wait?

"Sure, that sounds great," I replied, wanting to see his place and how he lived.

The drive over was quiet. Neither of us spoke but I could tell something was on his mind and troubling him. As we pulled into the parking lot of his apartment he quickly got out and ran over to my door to open it.

"Let's get in quickly before anyone sees you" He whispered.

We rushed inside and he quickly closed the door, handing me the remote to his T.V. "Now, just stay here. I won't be long." His tone was firm, almost commanding. As he reached the door, he turned to me, his expression serious. "And Sarah, don't open the door for anyone while I'm gone. It's important. You need to stay my secret for now, okay?"

His words sent a chill down my spine. "My secret"? The phrase echoed in my mind, a sinister undertone to what should have been a simple request. "Okay, Derik. I'll stay inside," I replied, though my voice was tinged with unease.

As the door closed behind him, I was left alone in the growing shadows of his apartment. The walls seemed to close in around me, the silence oppressive. Derik's behavior, his urgency, and his insistence on secrecy filled me with a sense of foreboding.

I walked to the window, gazing out at the quiet street. The world outside seemed a million miles away, a reality disconnected from the unsettling environment Derik had left me in. My thoughts raced, trying to piece together the puzzle of his actions, the cryptic nature of his visit.

His unfamiliar apartment felt like a cage, a space tainted by the unknown. I wrapped my arms around myself, a futile attempt to ward off the unsettling feeling that had settled in my chest.

As the evening grew later, the apartment grew darker, the shadows deeper. I was alone, yet the weight of Derik's presence lingered, an invisible specter in the room. I sat in the dim light, lost in a sea of troubling thoughts, my heart beating a frantic rhythm of apprehension and uncertainty. The sense of freedom I had felt earlier in the day had evaporated, replaced by a growing fear of what lay hidden in the darkness.

The silence of the apartment was abruptly shattered by a knock at the door. Heart pounding, I rose from the couch, expecting Derik's return. The heavy feeling in my chest twisted with a mix of anticipation and unease. I reached for the door handle, my hands trembling slightly.

As the door swung open, the figure I saw was not Derik. Instead, a woman stood there, her face etched with anger and distress, holding two small children close to her. "Are you Sarah?" she demanded, her voice sharp and accusing.

Confused and startled, I nodded, unable to find my voice.

"I'm Derik's wife," she said, the words hitting me like a physical blow. "What are you doing with my husband?"

Her revelation left me reeling. Derik's wife? The room seemed to spin around me as the implications of her words sank in. I stammered, trying to form a coherent response, but nothing made sense anymore.

Before I could reply, a car pulled up. Derik stepped out, his face contorting in anger as he saw us. Without a word, he marched up to the porch, his movements brusque and menacing.

"What are you doing here?" he barked at the woman, his voice laced with fury.

"Don't you dare, Derik! These are your children!" she cried, holding the children tighter to her. The fear in her eyes was palpable, a mirror of the dread building inside me.

In a sudden, violent motion, Derik shoved her off the porch, the children crying out in their mother's arms. I gasped, frozen in place, the scene unfolding before me like a nightmarish tableau.

"Get in your car and go home!" Derik yelled at her, his voice booming in the quiet street. The woman, clutching her children, scrambled to her feet and hurried to the car, her sobs echoing in the night air.

Once they were gone, Derik turned to me, his eyes

wild with rage. Before I could react, he was upon me, one hand gripping my arm and the other on my throat as he pinned me against the wall. His face was inches from mine, contorted with anger.

"Why did you open the door? I told you not to open the door!" he screamed, his breath hot against my skin.

I was petrified, trapped by his grip, and by the sudden, horrifying understanding of the situation. The man I thought I knew, the person I had trusted, was a stranger – dangerous and unpredictable.

"I... I thought it was you," I managed to choke out, my voice trembling with fear.

"You never listen! You're just like her!" Derik spat, his words laced with contempt. His grip tightened, the pressure building against my throat as I struggled to breathe.

In that moment, the illusion of freedom I had cherished shattered into a thousand pieces. The realization that I had stepped from one form of captivity into another was a bitter pill to swallow. I had left the constraints of the foster system only to find myself in the grasp of someone far more dangerous.

Derik's rage eventually subsided, and he released me, stepping back as if suddenly aware of his own actions. I slid down the wall, my body shaking, tears streaming down my face.

I laid there huddled on the floor, the weight of my choices and the reality of my situation crushing me. The freedom I had longed for, the independence I had sought, had led me here – to a place of fear and betrayal. As I sat there, with Derik standing above me in the dimly lit room, I realized that the path to true freedom was fraught with obstacles, some of which were of my own making. The journey ahead was uncertain, but one thing was clear – the choices I made from here on out would define not just my freedom, but also my very survival.

22 THE ASSAULT

After the nightmarish scene at the apartment, Derik's sudden shift from rage to remorse was disorienting. He extended his hand to me, a gesture that seemed so at odds with the fury I had just witnessed. Hesitantly, I let him help me to my feet, my body still trembling from the encounter.

"Let me drive you home," he said, his voice soft, almost pleading. I nodded, not trusting my voice, still processing the whirlwind of emotions.

The drive back to my house was filled with a tense air. Derik kept stealing glances at me, his eyes red and watery. "I'm so sorry, Sarah," he started, breaking the silence. "I don't know what came over me. I've never been like that before."

I sat quietly, listening, a part of me wanting to crawl away from his apologies, another part clinging to them. The Derik I knew was gentle and caring, not the man who had just unleashed such anger.

"My divorce... it's been hell," he continued, his voice breaking. "My ex, she's trying to turn my life upside down. She's... she's not stable. It's been tough, really tough."

I glanced at him, seeing the raw pain in his expression. It was difficult to reconcile this side of him with the man who had just lost control. "I understand it's hard," I managed to say, my voice small.

As we pulled up to my house, Derik reached over, taking my hand. "Can we start over? Please, I'm not that person you saw tonight."

I looked into his eyes, searching for the Derik I knew. After a moment of hesitation, I nodded. "Okay, but... we need to take things slow."

The following weeks were a whirlwind of emotions. Derik was like a man reborn, showering me with attention, laughter, and small gifts. We went on dates, watched movies, and walked in the park. He was the epitome of the perfect boyfriend, and for a while, I let myself get lost in the happiness he brought.

But beneath the surface, there was a constant undercurrent of fear, a reminder of the night that had shattered my trust. It lingered in the back of my mind, an unspoken shadow over our renewed relationship.

One evening, as we sat watching the sunset, Derik turned to me. "Sarah, I want to make things right. I want us to have a future together."

I smiled, but my heart was racing. "I want that too, Derik. But we need to be honest with each other, no more secrets."

He nodded, taking my hand. "No more secrets," he echoed.

The next morning, I called Derik to discuss our plans of going out that night. He didn't answer. Over the next several hours, I tried a few more times but nothing. He didn't show up that evening to pick me up and I fell asleep worried about what I may have done to upset him. Every possible scenario running through my head.

The sudden disappearance of Derik left a void in my life, an absence filled with confusion and hurt. His phone went straight to voicemail, and my texts lingered unanswered, floating in a digital limbo. In a desperate attempt to find answers, I went to his apartment, only to be greeted by the stark reality of its emptiness. The silence of the vacant rooms echoed my own feelings of abandonment. It was as if he had vanished, leaving no trace behind.

As the days turned into weeks, the sharp sting of Derik's absence began to dull. I found a job at a local gas station, a place far removed from the complexities of my recent past. It was mundane work, but in its simplicity, I found a sort of solace.

It was there that I met a group of people who would soon become my friends. They were blissfully unaware of the shadows that had trailed me, seeing me not as a victim of circumstances but as a peer, an equal. They drew me into their world – a world of laughter, parties, and the carefree joy of youth.

I still remember the night of my first party with them. The music was loud, a pulsating rhythm that filled the air with energy. People danced, talked, and laughed, a lively tapestry of life in motion. It was a stark contrast to the controlled environments I had been used to.

Amid the crowd, I noticed him – a guy with a genuine smile and a demeanor that radiated warmth. We struck up a conversation, his easy-going nature making me feel at ease. He talked about tedious things – movies, music, the weather – and I found myself caught up in the normalcy of it all.

As the party wound down, he hesitated for a moment before asking, "Would you like to go to the movies with me tomorrow night?"

I paused, surprised by the invitation. A part of me was still entangled in the mess with Derik, but another part yearned to move forward. "Yes, I'd like that," I replied, a smile breaking through my uncertainty.

That night, as I lay in bed, the events of the party replayed in my mind. It felt like a turning point, a step away from the chaos of my past and towards something new, something hopeful.

Derik, who had once been my anchor, had drifted away, leaving me adrift. But now, I was beginning to find my own way, navigating the waters of life with a newfound sense of freedom.

The next evening as I was preparing for the movie date, a sense of excitement mingled with apprehension came over me. It was a new beginning, a chance to redefine myself away from the shadows of my past. As I looked at my reflection in the mirror, I saw not just Sarah, but the possibilities of who I could become – stronger, wiser, and in control of my own story.

The excitement of my impending date was like a breath of fresh air, a feeling I had not experienced in what felt like a lifetime. I was just slipping on my jacket, a smile playing on my lips, when the unexpected sound of my door being forced open caused me to freeze in shock.

There, in the doorway, stood Derik. His eyes were wild, his stance aggressive, exuding an energy that was both frightening and disconcerting.

"Derik! What are you doing here?" I stammered, my heart racing.

"I saw you, getting ready. Who are you going out with?" His voice was accusatory, his gaze piercing.

"I have a date," I said, my voice steadier than I felt. "You can't just barge in here like this, Derik."

"A date?" His voice rose in pitch, a dangerous edge creeping into his tone. "You're mine, Sarah. You can't just go out with someone else."

His words sent a chill through me. The possessiveness in his voice was unmistakable, a stark reminder of the unsettling undercurrents that had always been part of our relationship.

"No, Derik. I'm not yours. You can't control me like this," I countered, trying to keep the fear out of my voice.

For a moment, he just stood there, his chest heaving, a storm of emotions playing across his face. Then, he lunged towards me, grabbing me by the shoulders and forcing me back towards my bedroom.

I tried to break free from his grip, but to no avail. He drug me through the doorway and threw me down on my bed.

"You will always be mine, Sarah!" he screamed while removing the belt from his jeans.

I jumped back towards him throwing with me, my full body weight, trying to knock him over but it felt as though I hit a brick wall. He squeezed my arms with a vice-like grip and shoved me back down, his own body crashing down on top of me.

As I laid there, the adrenaline slowly ebbing from my veins, I realized the magnitude of what was happening and just like when I was younger, back at home with my stepfather, I closed my eyes and allowed my mind to wander to another place.

23 SEEKING LIGHT IN THE DARK

The days following my horrifying encounter with Derik turned into a blur of desolation. I watched as the world outside continued to move, the sun rising and setting with its usual rhythm, but for me, time seemed to stand still. My small house, once a haven of freedom and new beginnings, now felt like a dungeon – its walls enclosing me in a world tinted with despair.

I remember staring at my phone as it rang, the name of my boss flashing on the screen. With each call, I mustered just enough strength to weave another excuse. "I'm sorry, I've come down with something quite bad," I murmured during one call, my voice a faint echo of its usual self.

The silence that followed my words was filled with unspoken questions, but I couldn't bring myself to say more. As soon as the call ended, I let the phone slip from my hands, the device landing softly on the couch – my only connection to the outside world, now discarded.

My friends tried to reach out, their messages and calls piling up in my inbox. "Sarah, are you okay?" one text read. "We haven't seen you in days," said another. But the thought of replying, of painting on a façade of normalcy, was overwhelmingly exhausting. I let the phone buzz and beep with incoming alerts, each one a reminder of the life I was now disconnected from.

Food became a mere necessity, each bite a tasteless chore. I would push the food around my plate, my appetite stolen by the heavy blanket of depression that had settled over me. The nights were the hardest. Sleep, once a sweet escape, now betrayed me. I would toss and turn, my mind replaying the events with Derik over and over. His body crushing mine, taking away every last bit of control, would appear in my dreams, jolting me awake, heart racing, a silent scream trapped in my throat.

The mirror in my bathroom reflected a stranger. Hollow eyes, a pale complexion, hair unkempt – the girl who looked back at me was a shadow of who I used to be. I often found myself whispering to her, "What happened to you, Sarah?"

The loneliness was palpable, a returning companion

in the empty house I now found myself in. I would sit by the window, watching life go on as if nothing had happened, as if my world hadn't come crashing down. The chirping of birds, the laughter of children playing outside – they all seemed like echoes from a different universe.

One evening, as the sun dipped below the horizon, casting long shadows across the room, I sat on the floor, the cold tiles against my skin offering a strange sense of comfort. My gaze fell on a photograph on the shelf – a picture of a happier time, a reminder of what once was.

As I reached out to touch the frame, a tear escaped, tracing a slow path down my cheek. It was in that moment, surrounded by the growing darkness, that the full weight of my solitude hit me. I was alone, utterly alone, lost in a universe of my own despair, with no land in sight.

The silence in my house was deafening, a stark contrast to the chaos that had just a week prior filled it. I kept to myself, the weight of what Derik did to me, a heavy shroud around my shoulders. I couldn't bring myself to share it, to voice the reality of that night. The fear and shame were too much, building walls of solitude that seemed impenetrable.

Days merged into nights, each indistinguishable from the last, until one night, something shifted. In the depths of a restless sleep, a dream broke through the darkness that had enveloped me. It was Michael, my teenage boyfriend from the hospital, who had passed away, leaving a void in my heart. In the dream, he was as I remembered – kind, smiling, a source of light in the gloom of my life.

"Sarah," he said, his voice cutting through the fog in my mind, "you deserve happiness. There are great things waiting for you."

His words, simple yet profound, echoed in the dream, reaching into the depths of my despair. When I awoke, the remnants of his voice still lingered, a soothing balm on my wounded soul.

For the first time in what felt like forever, a spark of hope flickered within me. It was faint, but it was there – a tiny lighthouse in the vast darkness. Clutching onto this newfound feeling, I found the strength to pick up my phone. My fingers trembled as I dialed my mother's number, each ring amplifying the anxiety within me.

"Mom," I started, my voice shaky, the words catching in my throat. "I... I need your help. I don't want to live here anymore. Can you come get me?"

There was a brief silence on the other end, and then, "Sarah, honey, are you okay?" Her voice was laced with worry, a mother's instinct kicking in.

I swallowed hard, fighting back the tears. "No, Mom, I'm not okay. I need to leave this place. I need to be closer to you, to start over."

There was a rustling sound, as if she was getting ready to leave immediately. "I'll be there as soon as I can. Just hang tight, sweetie. We'll figure this out together."

Hanging up the phone, I felt a sense of relief wash over me. It was as if admitting my need for help, reaching out to my mother, had lifted a part of the burden I had been carrying. The walls of my self-imposed isolation began to crumble, letting in the light of hope and the possibility of healing.

As I waited for her to come, I sat by the window, watching the sky turn from black to shades of blue. Dawn was approaching, its light a symbol of the new beginning that awaited me. The pain and fear were still there, but now, there was also a path forward, a chance to rebuild and find the happiness that Michael had spoken of in my dream. It was the end of one chapter, but the start of another – a journey towards healing, understanding, and ultimately, self-rediscovery.

As the sound of the truck's engine hummed softly in the background, my mother and her friend Beth's arrival marked the end of an era in my life. I greeted them with a small, tentative smile.

"Sarah, how are you holding up?" my mother asked, her voice laced with concern as she stepped through the door.

"I'm managing, Mom," I replied, trying to sound more assured than I felt. "I just... I need to be closer to you all now."

She nodded, understandingly, her eyes scanning the room, taking in the bare walls and packed boxes. "We're here for you, sweetheart. Always," she said, her tone gentle.

Beth, in her usual effort to lighten the mood, chimed in, "Looks like you're all set to make a move, huh? A new start can be exciting!"

I forced a smile at her comment, appreciating her attempt to bring some normalcy to the situation.

As we began packing up the remnants of my life in the empty house, Beth stumbled upon the broken bedframe. Her eyes twinkled with mischief as she made a lighthearted comment, "Whoa, what happened here? Did you have a wrestling match or something?"

The joke hit too close to home. I felt a sudden tightness in my chest, my breath hitching slightly. I quickly turned my face away to hide my reaction, busying myself with a nearby box. "Yeah, something like that," I managed to say, my voice a whisper.

"Hey, it's okay. New beginnings, right?" Beth said, sensing she might have touched a nerve.

My mother gave me a knowing look but didn't press further. She understood my need for privacy, for dealing with things in my own time.

As we carried the boxes to the truck, my mother spoke softly, "We'll find you a nice place, Sarah. Somewhere you can feel safe and start rebuilding."

I nodded, grateful for her support. "Thanks, Mom. I just want to be near family again. I think it will help," I said, feeling the weight of my unspoken truths.

I squeezed her hand, a silent thank you. In that moment, I realized that while I was leaving behind a chapter filled with pain and darkness, I was also moving towards a future where hope and healing were possible.

My mother stepped forward and enveloped me in a hug. It was warm, filled with the love and relief that only a mother could provide. "Of course, Sarah. We're here for you," she said, her voice a soothing balm to my frayed nerves.

As we loaded the last of my belongings into the truck, my mother talked about the future. "We'll find you a nice place close to us. A fresh start," she said, optimism lacing her words.

I nodded, grateful for her support yet weighed down by the guilt of my silence. The decision to keep the secret of that night was a heavy one, but I wasn't ready to unravel those threads. Not yet.

Standing at the threshold of the now-empty house, I took one last look around. The walls, once blank canvases, had witnessed the highs and lows of my life here. They had seen my dreams, my fears, and now, they were privy to my silent suffering.

As we drove away, the neighborhood growing smaller in the rearview mirror, I felt a mixture of sorrow and relief. I was leaving behind a significant chapter of my life, one that had shaped me in ways I was still understanding.

I gazed out of the truck window, watching the familiar streets pass by. I was heading towards a future unknown, but with a sense of hope that had been rekindled in me. It was a hope not just for a place to live, but for healing, for rediscovering the strength within myself, and for the chance to build a life that was truly my own.

24 A NEW BEGINNING

As I stepped into the bright yellow house, its walls radiating a warm, welcoming glow, I felt a surge of excitement. This wasn't just a new house; it was a symbol of a new chapter in my life, starkly different from the dim, cramped spaces I had left behind. Unpacking my belongings, I felt a deep sense of ownership and possibility with each item I set in place.

"Quite the cheerful spot you've picked, Sarah," my mom remarked, her voice filled with a mixture of pride and affection as she entered, followed closely by Andrew, her boyfriend. He carried a large plant, its leaves adding a touch of life to the room.

"It feels right, Mom," I responded, taking the plant from Andrew and finding the perfect spot for it near the window. "Thanks for bringing this."

Behind them, my teenage siblings, Lily and Henry, burst through the door, their energy and curiosity filling the space instantly. Lily, ever the explorer, began examining every corner of the house, while Henry, more reserved, carefully inspected the bookshelves I had just set up.

"Where do you want this, Sarah?" Andrew asked, gesturing to a box marked 'Kitchen Stuff.'

"Just over there is fine," I directed, pointing to the kitchen. His presence in my family's lives had brought a sense of stability and warmth, and I was grateful for his help today.

As we all worked together, the house began to transform from an empty space into something that felt like a home. Mom hung some pictures on the walls, Andrew assembled furniture with an ease that spoke of experience, and Lily and Henry found ways to make themselves useful, even if it was just arranging the cushions on the sofa.

Taking a moment to step back, I watched my family moving around, interacting with each other in this new space that was mine. There was a sense of peace that washed over me, a feeling that up until now, had seemed so foreign.

My phone rang, pulling me away from the commotion. It was John, my older brother, calling from the next town over.

"Hey, John," I answered, stepping into the newfound quiet of my bedroom.

"Sarah! How's the move going?" His voice was always a comforting blend of enthusiasm and calm.

"It's going great. Mom, Andrew, Lily, and Henry are all here helping. We just wish you were here too."

"I'll make it over next weekend. Can't wait to see your new place. How are you settling in?"

"Better than I expected. It feels like... like I'm finally home."

After the call, I returned to the living room, where the sounds of my family echoed gently off the walls. In the following days, I spent my time decorating, each touch a reflection of my journey and growth. The house slowly filled with my personality and my new dreams.

The morning sun cast a golden hue over the neighborhood as I stood by the kitchen window one Friday morning, sipping my coffee. It was in this tranquil moment that I first saw him – the soldier from next door. He was in his front yard, his back turned to me, his posture speaking of discipline and strength. Even from a distance, there was a certain air about him, a mix of mystery and an unspoken story that piqued my curiosity. I found myself drawn to the window each morning, subtly watching him go about his routine. There was something about him, perhaps the way he moved or the rare moments he paused to gaze at the sky, that stirred a feeling within me, a crush I hadn't anticipated.

Later that week, I decided it was time for a new addition to my life – a pet. I found myself at the local animal shelter, where a small, white rabbit with curious eyes caught my attention. As I held it gently, feeling its soft fur and the quiet thump of its heart, I knew it was the companion I had been seeking.

Bringing it home, I set up a large cage in the backyard, taking care to make it comfortable and inviting. As I arranged its new home, I talked to it softly, "You're going to like it here, little one. We're both starting over, in a way."

The rabbit, which I decided to call Marbles due to its round, expressive eyes, hopped around its new space, exploring eagerly. Watching Marbles settle in, I felt a connection to this tiny creature, a shared sense of beginning anew.

Later that evening, as I sat outside watching Marbles explore his new home, I reflected on the changes in my life. The move, the new house, my growing family bond, and now Marbles – each piece was a step towards something new, something hopeful. It was in this moment of contemplation that I realized how much I had grown, how the challenges of my past had shaped me into who I was now. I was no longer the person who felt lost and adrift; I was someone who had found her place, her peace.

As the sun set, casting long shadows across the yard, I felt a contentment that was new and deeply comforting. The pieces of my life were coming together in this little yellow house, each one a fragment of the new world I was building for myself. And as I looked out at the quiet street, the mysterious soldier from next door briefly crossed my mind, a reminder of the possibilities that lay just beyond my front door.

One crisp morning, while I was outside tending to Marbles, a soft voice interrupted my thoughts. "Is that your bunny?" I looked up to see a little girl from next door, her eyes wide with curiosity as she peered through the fence.

"Yes, it is," I replied, smiling at her innocence. "His name is Marbles."

"I'm Emily," she said, a shy smile creeping onto her face. "Can I come see him?"

"Of course, Emily," I said, opening a small gate in the fence. She came through cautiously, her gaze fixed on Marbles with a child's unfiltered fascination.

"He's so fluffy!" Emily exclaimed, her voice a mixture of awe and delight as she gently stroked Marbles under my supervision.

"Do you have any pets, Emily?" I asked, enjoying her company.

"We used to have a dog, but not anymore. My big brother said we might get another one when he's home more," she replied, her small fingers carefully petting Marbles.

"Your big brother?" I inquired, a hint of curiosity in my voice.

"Yeah, he's a soldier. He just got back from being away for a long time!" Her voice was tinged with pride and a hint of relief.

"A soldier?" I echoed, the pieces clicking together in my mind. The mysterious figure I'd seen was her brother.

The next day, as I was watering the plants in my front yard, I heard a voice from the other side of the fence. "Hi, there. I'm Jake, Emily's brother." I turned to see the soldier standing there, a friendly smile on his face. He was taller than I had imagined, with a presence that was both quiet and gentle.

"Hi, Jake. I'm Sarah. Emily came over yesterday to meet my rabbit," I responded, feeling a flutter of nervous excitement.

"I heard about that. She hasn't stopped talking about Marbles. I wanted to thank you for being so kind to her," he said, his voice warm and genuine.

"It was my pleasure. She's a sweet girl," I replied, tucking a strand of hair behind my ear, a nervous habit.

"Listen, I'm having a few friends over for drinks tonight at my parent's place. Would you like to come? Nothing fancy, just a casual hangout," he invited, his eyes holding a friendly invitation.

I hesitated for a moment, the unexpected invitation

catching me off guard. But looking into his sincere eyes, I felt a sense of daring, a desire to step out of my comfort zone.

"Sure, that sounds nice. I'd like that," I found myself saying, surprised at my own boldness.

"Great! Come over around seven?" he suggested.

"Seven works for me," I confirmed, a smile playing on my lips.

As he walked away, I felt a mixture of anticipation and nerves. This was new territory for me, stepping into a social scene, especially one that involved the intriguing soldier next door. But as I looked back at my cheerful yellow house, I realized this was part of my journey - opening up to new experiences and connections. Tonight was just another step in my ever-evolving path.

At seven, I found myself standing nervously at Jake's front door, a bottle of wine in hand as a gesture of thanks. Taking a deep breath, I rang the bell. The door swung open, revealing Jake with a warm, inviting smile.

"Hey, Sarah, glad you could make it. Come on in," he said, stepping aside to let me in.

The interior of his house was cozy and lived-in, with comfortable furniture and personal touches that made it feel welcoming. A small group of people were gathered in the living room, laughing and talking. Jake introduced me to each of them, and I was struck by how genuinely friendly they all were.

As the evening progressed, I found myself relaxing into the atmosphere. Jake was an attentive host, making sure everyone was comfortable, including me. Our conversations flowed easily, covering everything from our neighborhood to our hobbies. I learned that he loved photography, and his passion for it was evident in the way his eyes lit up when he spoke about his travels and the shots he captured.

There were moments throughout the night when our eyes met, and a silent understanding passed between us. It was as if we were both acknowledging the budding connection, unsure but intrigued by its potential.

In the days that followed, Jake and I found more opportunities to talk. He would often be outside when I was tending to Marbles or working in the garden. Our conversations were casual but increasingly filled with laughter and shared stories.

One afternoon, I struggled to hang a new light fixture outside my front door. Jake noticed and came over to help. "Need a hand with that?" he asked, a teasing glimmer in his eyes.

"Actually, yes, that would be great," I admitted, grateful for his assistance.

Working together, we managed to get the light fixed. "There," he said, stepping back to admire our handiwork. "Looks good."

"Thanks, Jake. I really appreciate the help," I said, feeling a warmth that had little to do with the task at hand.

It wasn't just our interactions that drew me to him. Watching him with Emily, the way he treated her with such gentle care and attention, revealed a softness in him that was deeply appealing.

Each encounter, each shared moment, seemed to weave a thread between us, connecting us in ways I hadn't anticipated. It was a slow, gradual process, a dance of getting to know each other, of exploring the possibility that lay between us.

As I lay in bed that night, I realized how much my life had changed since moving into the yellow house. New beginnings, new connections, and now, a new potential chapter with Jake. It was exciting and a little daunting, but I felt ready for whatever lay ahead. The growth I had experienced, the peace I had found in my new home, and now the thrill of a budding relationship – it was a journey I never expected but one I was wholeheartedly embracing.

25 A LOVE THAT UNDERSTANDS

Standing in the quiet, unassuming barracks where Jake spent much of his time, I was acutely aware of the significance of this moment. The walls, usually echoing with the sounds of discipline and duty, were now silent witnesses to a softer, more intimate scene. Jake took my hands in his, his eyes reflecting a depth of emotion that resonated with my own.

"Sarah," he began, his voice steady yet laden with emotion, "these past months with you have been the most transformative of my life. You've shown me a love that is deep, honest, and full of understanding."

I felt a surge of emotion, a mix of anticipation and a deep-seated joy. The room around us seemed to fade, leaving just the two of us, standing in our own little world.

"Sarah, I want to spend my life with you, learning from you, growing with you. Will you marry me?" His words were simple, but they carried the weight of a thousand promises.

Tears welled in my eyes, not of sorrow, but of an overwhelming sense of love and belonging. "Yes, Jake. Yes, I will marry you," I whispered, my voice barely audible over the pounding of my heart.

As he slipped the ring onto my finger, a symbol of our commitment, I realized that this was more than a proposal. It was a recognition of our journey together, a journey that had brought healing and hope.

The weeks that followed were a whirlwind of wedding preparations. We found ourselves immersed in a sea of decisions - venues, guest lists, color schemes. But each choice we made was a reflection of our partnership, a blend of our personalities and preferences.

"Maybe a small, intimate ceremony?" I suggested one evening as we sat surrounded by brochures and notes.

Jake looked up from a list he was scribbling on. "I like that idea. Let's keep it personal and meaningful."

My family was a constant source of support. My

mother and my aunt, with their impeccable taste, offered to help with the decorations. Lily and Henri, now brimming with teenage enthusiasm, volunteered to be a part of the bridal party. And in a touching gesture, Jake's sister Emily eagerly offered to be our flower girl.

However, amidst the joy, there were moments of stress and compromise. Jake and I had our differences, but we navigated them with open communication and a deep respect for each other's viewpoints.

"What about the music for the reception?" Jake asked during one of our planning sessions.

"I was thinking something classic, maybe a live band?" I countered, hoping he would agree.

He pondered for a moment, then nodded. "Sounds perfect. Let's do it."

As the day of our wedding drew closer, the excitement was palpable. But more than the excitement, there was a sense of rightness, a feeling that every step we had taken was leading us to this moment of union.

Amid the chaos of planning, I often found myself pausing, reflecting on the journey that had brought me here. From the loneliness and struggles of my past to the love and companionship I now shared with Jake, it was a testament to the unpredictable, yet beautiful, nature of life.

Our wedding wasn't just a celebration of our love; it was a celebration of growth, of overcoming, and of finding peace in the arms of another. It was the start of a new chapter, one that Jake and I would write together, with all its challenges and joys. As I looked forward to the day I would walk down the aisle towards him, I knew in my heart that this was exactly where I was meant to be.

The morning of our wedding dawned bright and clear, a perfect mirror to the joy and anticipation I felt inside. As I dressed in my simple yet elegant gown given to me by Jake's mother, I couldn't help but reflect on the journey that had brought me to this moment. It was a day not just to celebrate my union with Jake but also to honor the personal growth that had paved the way to where I stand now.

The ceremony was beautiful, set in a small building filled with flowers and the gentle whispers of family and close friends. The love and support from my family were palpable, their smiles and tears a testament to the bond we shared. Jake looked handsome and serene, waiting for me at the end of the aisle, his eyes shining with emotion.

However, I couldn't help but notice the reserved demeanor of Jake's family. Their polite smiles didn't quite reach their eyes, and their congratulations were formal, lacking warmth. It was clear that they held reservations about me, but I chose not to let it overshadow our day. This was about the love Jake and I shared, a love strong enough to weather any external disapproval.

As newlyweds, Jake and I settled into a life that was both comforting and exhilarating. We found joy in the simple act of setting up our home, each item we placed carrying a piece of our shared story.

One evening, as we arranged the living room, Jake paused, holding a framed photograph of us. "I think this should go right here, where we can always see it," he said, placing it on the end table.

"That's perfect," I replied, admiring how the photo captured a moment of genuine happiness.

Our daily routines became moments of connection. Mornings often found us in the kitchen, Jake making coffee while I prepared breakfast. We'd talk about our plans for the day, our conversations filled with laughter and shared dreams.

"Hey, I was thinking we could try that new restaurant this weekend," Jake suggested one morning, his hand finding mine across the kitchen counter.

"I'd love that," I responded, excited at the prospect of exploring something so simple but new together.

Evenings were our time to unwind and reconnect. We'd often sit on the porch, watching the sunset, talking about everything and nothing. These moments, simple in their essence, were the building blocks of our life together.

"Today was good," Jake would say, his arm around me as we watched the sky turn from blue to hues of orange and pink.

"It was," I'd agree, feeling a sense of contentment that was new to me.

Despite the initial coolness from Jake's family, our life was a testament to the love and understanding we shared. We supported each other's aspirations, celebrated each other's successes, and provided comfort during challenges. Our relationship was a constant reminder of the beauty and strength that comes from a partnership based on mutual respect and deep love.

The early days of our marriage, though filled with love and shared happiness, were not without their challenges. The most persistent of these stemmed from the way Jake's family treated me. Their coolness, once something I could overlook, began to create a subtle tension between Jake and me.

One evening, as we sat on the porch, the issue finally came to a head. "Jake, I feel like your family still hasn't accepted me," I admitted, the words tasting bitter in my mouth.

Jake sighed, a look of concern crossing his face. "I know, Sarah. I've seen it too. It's not fair to you. I'm sorry."

"It's not your fault," I reassured him. "But it does hurt. It feels like they're waiting for me to fail."

Jake took my hand, his grip firm and reassuring. "I'll talk to them, Sarah. We're in this together, and you deserve to be treated with respect and love."

His words were a balm, soothing the sting of rejection I had felt. It was moments like this that reinforced the strength of our bond, our ability to face challenges together and come out stronger.

Our shared interests and activities played a significant role in strengthening our bond. One of the things we both came to enjoy was attending concerts together. Jake introduced me to Lamb of God and Megadeth, bands he loved and I soon began to appreciate.

At our first concert together, the energy of the crowd was infectious. "This is incredible!" I shouted over the roar of the music, a wide grin on my face.

Jake laughed, his eyes alight with excitement. "Told you you'd love it!"

The concerts became our thing, a way to let loose and enjoy our shared love for music. It was a side of Jake I cherished, and my growing enjoyment of the music was something we both celebrated.

Supporting each other's dreams was another cornerstone of our marriage. My career in healthcare was demanding but fulfilling, and Jake's encouragement was unwavering.

"You're doing amazing work, Sarah," he would say, his pride evident in his voice. "I'm so proud of you."

Jake's passion for music, particularly his guitar playing, was something I supported wholeheartedly. "You should play more often," I often encouraged him. "You have a real talent."

It was in these moments, supporting each other's aspirations, that our love and understanding for each other deepened. We weren't just husband and wife; we were partners in every sense of the word, champions of each other's dreams and aspirations.

As we navigated the complexities of our life together, facing challenges and embracing our shared interests, our relationship evolved into something profoundly beautiful. It was a testament to the fact that love when paired with respect, communication, and mutual support, could overcome any obstacle, and make any joy that much sweeter.

In the quiet solitude of our bedroom, I often found myself reflecting on the journey that had led me here. Turning the pages of my diary, I wrote about the profound impact Jake had on my life. "With Jake, I've found not just love, but healing," I penned. "He understands the scars of my past and stands with me as I heal. Together, we're building a life filled with hope."

These moments of introspection were crucial. They allowed me to see how far I had come - from the shadows of my past to the light of a future filled with love and understanding.

Our life together was marked by celebrations, big and small. Each milestone, whether personal or professional, was a testament to our growth and progress as a couple. Jake's leaving the Army was one such occasion. I was shocked at first, hearing the news but we decided to celebrate the coming chapter in his life and moved back to be closer to family.

"I know it wasn't an easy decision, but, I'm proud of you for making the decision to do what's best for you," I toasted, raising my glass. His smile, full of gratitude and love, was all I needed to see.

We also celebrated my achievements in healthcare, each step forward a reminder of my passion and commitment to helping others. Jake was always there, cheering me on, his belief in me unwavering.

"These are the moments that make life worthwhile," he would say, his arm wrapped around me as we shared our successes and dreams.

The chapter of our life together culminated in a quiet evening at home, a simple yet profound celebration of our love and partnership. Surrounded by the warmth of our living room, with soft music playing in the background, we reminisced about the journey we had shared.

"You know, Sarah, every day with you is a reminder of how powerful love can be," Jake said, his eyes meeting mine across the room.

"I feel the same way," I replied, my heart full. "You've brought so much light into my life."

It was moments like these that encapsulated the essence of our relationship - a partnership rooted in mutual respect, understanding, and a deep, healing love.

As we sat there, lost in conversation and laughter, I realized that our love was more than just a feeling. It was a force, a driving power that had brought healing and hope not only to me but to both of us. We were partners in the truest sense, navigating life's ups and downs together, always moving forward, always growing.

This chapter of our story was just one of many, but it was a vital one. It laid the foundation for a future where love and healing were intertwined, where every challenge was faced with unity, and every joy was amplified by our shared journey. In Jake, I had found more than a husband; I had found a partner in life, a beacon of hope, and a testament to the enduring power of love.

.

26 UNEXPECTED TURNS

Sitting in the small, impersonal doctor's office, I anxiously tapped my foot, my mind a whirlwind of worry over what I assumed was just a stubborn flu. The doctor's entry broke my reverie, her expression unreadable as she held my test results.

"Sarah, your tests are back, and it's not the flu," she began, her voice calm and professional. My heart skipped a beat, bracing for bad news. "You're pregnant."

Pregnant? The word echoed in my mind, a mix of disbelief and wonder washing over me. I was unprepared for this revelation, my emotions a tangled web of joy, shock, and a faint, nagging fear.

"Are you sure?" I managed to ask, my voice barely above a whisper.

"Quite sure," she replied with a gentle smile. "Congratulations, Sarah."

The drive home was a blur. I was about to embark on a journey I had never anticipated. How would Jake react? Were we ready for this?

As I stepped through the door, Jake's concerned face greeted me. "Hey, everything okay? You look like you've seen a ghost."

"Jake, I'm... we're going to have a baby," I said, the words feeling surreal even as they left my mouth.

His initial shock mirrored mine, quickly transforming into a wide, joyous smile. "Really? That's... that's amazing, Sarah!" He pulled me into a warm embrace, our shared excitement tangible in the air.

"We're going to be parents," I murmured, a smile breaking through my initial shock.

That night, we lay together, talking about future plans, names, and all the possibilities that lay ahead. It was a beautiful, tender moment, a bubble of happiness amidst the uncertainty of life.

However, as my pregnancy progressed, so did my internal struggles. My nights were plagued with nightmares, echoes of my past fears, and anxieties. I dreamt of being a mother, but in these dreams, I was always failing, always falling short. The vivid images of me being unable to protect my child haunted me, stirring doubts about my capability as a mother.

I confided in Jake one night, my voice trembling as I recounted the nightmares. "I'm scared, Jake. What if I'm not a good mother? What if I can't protect our child?"

He held me close, his presence a comforting anchor in the storm of my fears. "Sarah, you're going to be an amazing mother. You're strong, loving, and caring. We'll figure this out together, I promise."

His words were reassuring, but the seed of doubt remained, nestled deep in my heart. I knew this was a hurdle I had to overcome, not just for my sake but for our child's as well. As I lay awake, Jake's steady breathing beside me, I realized that this journey of motherhood would be one of learning and growing, of facing my fears and embracing the unknown.

This chapter of my life, unexpected and daunting as it was, was also a chance for growth and healing. It was a challenge I was determined to meet head-on, armed with love, support, and a newfound strength I was only just beginning to discover.

The joy and anticipation of our upcoming arrival were soon tempered by a growing tension between Jake and me. It began subtly, a slight shift in our conversations, but gradually escalated into a significant point of contention.

One evening, as we sat down to discuss our plans for the future, Jake dropped a bombshell. "I've been thinking a lot about this, Sarah. I want to quit my job and stay home with the baby."

I stared at him, disbelief coloring my tone. "Quit your job? Jake, we need the income, especially with a baby on the way."

He leaned forward, his expression earnest. "I know, but this is important to me. I want to be there for our child in a way my dad never was for me."

I understood where he was coming from, but the practical side of me was reeling. "We've planned our finances based on two incomes. How can we just change everything now?"

Our conversations soon turned into arguments, each of us entrenched in our perspectives. The stress of the pregnancy, coupled with this disagreement, began to take a toll on our relationship.

"I just feel like you're not seeing how important this is to me," Jake said during one of our heated discussions, frustration evident in his voice.

"And you're not seeing how risky this is," I shot back, the weight of my own fears making me defensive.

It felt like we were at an impasse, each argument leaving a deeper crack in the foundation of our relationship.

After days of turmoil and sleepless nights, I found myself sitting alone in the nursery, lost in thought. The realization slowly dawned on me that perhaps there was more at stake here than just our financial security. This was about supporting each other's needs and dreams.

The next day, I approached Jake with a decision that had taken me countless hours to reach. "Jake, I've been thinking. I don't want our child to grow up in a home filled with tension. If this is what you truly want, then I support you in quitting your job."

He looked at me, a mix of surprise and relief in his eyes. "Are you sure, Sarah? I know this isn't what you wanted."

"I'm sure," I said, a sense of resolve in my voice. "We'll make it work. Our family and our happiness come first."

The aftermath of my decision was a period of adjustment. We sat down together, pouring over our finances, making budgets, and planning for a future that looked very different from what we had initially envisioned.

"I'll sell some of my things," Jake offered, determined to contribute financially in some way. "And I'll take care of the house and the baby. We can balance it out."

I nodded, appreciative of his willingness to find a middle ground. "And I'll continue working. We'll just have to be a bit more careful with our expenses."

As we reorganized our lives around this significant change, I couldn't help but feel a mix of apprehension and hope. Giving up the security of two incomes was daunting, but in its place, we were building a new kind of security - one rooted in mutual support and understanding.

This chapter of our lives was not just about the

arrival of our child, but also about redefining our relationship and priorities. It was a testament to the power of compromise and the strength of our commitment to each other. As I watched Jake, his face lit up with enthusiasm for his new role, I knew that despite the challenges, we were on the right path, a path paved with love, sacrifice, and a deep trust in each other.

The shift in our dynamic, brought on by the decision for Jake to stay at home, gradually eased as we began the tangible preparations for our baby's arrival. The nursery, once an empty room, slowly transformed into a haven of love and anticipation. We painted the walls a gentle blue, laughing at our ineptitude with the brushes, our earlier tensions melting away in these moments of shared purpose.

"I think he'll like this," Jake said one day, holding up a mobile of stars and planets. We had just learned we were having a boy, a revelation that brought a new wave of excitement.

"He will," I agreed, imagining our son gazing up at the twinkling shapes.

As we folded tiny clothes and arranged soft toys, we talked about our hopes and fears for parenthood. "I

just want to be there for him, in every way I can,"
Jake expressed one evening, his voice tinged with
determination.

"And you will be," I assured him, my hand resting
on my growing belly. "We both will."

In the quiet hours of the night, I often found myself
alone with my thoughts. Lying in bed, I reflected on
the incredible journey my life had taken since
meeting Jake. From the depths of past traumas to
the unexpected twists of love and now the brink of
motherhood, it was a path marked by growth and
resilience. This pregnancy, while fraught with its
own set of fears, was also a beacon of hope, a
tangible symbol of the new life we were building
together.

I thought about my nightmares, the fears of not
being enough, and realized that they were just
shadows compared to the strength and love I had
found in myself and in my relationship with Jake.
This was a new phase, one that would undoubtedly
test us, but also one that promised so much joy and
fulfillment.

One evening as Jake and I sat together in the completed nursery. The room was peaceful, bathed in the soft glow of the evening light. We sat side by side, my head resting on his shoulder, both lost in thoughts of the future.

"Do you think we're ready for this?" I asked quietly, a mix of anticipation and nervousness in my voice.

Jake squeezed my hand, a gesture filled with reassurance. "As ready as we'll ever be. We're doing this together, and that's what matters."

I looked around the nursery, at the crib that stood ready, the shelves lined with books and toys, and felt a profound sense of peace. Despite the challenges we had faced and the ones yet to come, I knew we were stepping into this new chapter with a renewed sense of unity and love.

"We're going to be okay, aren't we?" I murmured, more to myself than to Jake.

"We are," he replied, his voice steady and sure. "We're going to be more than okay."

In that moment, there was nothing but hope and the quiet anticipation of the life that was about to begin. It was a moment of stillness, a deep breath before the plunge into the unknown waters of parenthood. And as I leaned into Jake, I realized that no matter what the future held, we would face it together, with love as our guiding light.

27 HORIZON OF HOPE

In the stark, bustling room of the hospital, surrounded by a symphony of clinical sounds and under the harsh glare of fluorescent lights, I lay engulfed in a tempest of pain and fear. Each surge of agony brought me closer to a transformative moment, a rebirth of sorts. Clinging to Jake's hand, I found an anchor in his steadfast presence, a source of strength amidst the chaos.

"Keep breathing, Sarah. You're almost there," the doctor encouraged, her voice firm yet reassuring, guiding me through the intense pain. I was teetering on the brink of a monumental change, at the edge of embracing a new identity.

With a final push, drawn from the depths of my soul, the room filled with the most primal and pure sound - my son's first cry. It was the sound of a new beginning, the first vocal testament to his existence in this world. Exhausted but exhilarated, I lay back, eagerly awaiting the culmination of months of anticipation and years of fears deeply rooted in my past.

As the nurse gently placed the tiny, wriggling bundle in my arms, a tidal wave of emotions overwhelmed me. Holding my son, feeling his delicate weight, everything felt profoundly natural and right. His eyes, bright and inquisitive, met mine, and in that instant, a profound shift occurred within me. My heart expanded with a fierce, protective love, eclipsing all previous apprehensions. He was here, he was mine, and he was perfect.

"Hello, my little one," I whispered, tears of joy and relief mingling on my cheeks. "I'm your mom, and I promise to always be here for you, to protect you."

In those first, fragile moments, as his tiny fingers curled around mine, a solemn vow formed in my heart. I committed to loving him unconditionally, to shielding him from the shadows of my own past, to laying a foundation of unwavering support and affection. I would be the mother I feared I couldn't be, the guardian of his innocence, the architect of his joy.

Jake, standing beside us with tears glistening in his eyes, whispered, "He's perfect, Sarah. Just like you.

We've created something beautiful."

"We have," I agreed, my voice imbued with wonder and newfound determination. Gazing into Jake's eyes, I saw not only the man I loved but also a partner in this incredible journey of parenthood we were embarking on.

As I cradled my son, feeling his warmth and the rhythmic rise and fall of his chest, I reflected on the path that had led me here. From the turbulent waters of a troubled past, through trials and tribulations, I had arrived at this pinnacle of joy - a testament to the resilience of the human spirit, my spirit.

This tiny being in my arms was not just the beginning of a new life but a beacon of hope, symbolizing the breaking of old cycles and the dawn of new legacies. His presence instilled in me a newfound strength, an unshakable resolve to provide a life brimming with love, understanding, and endless opportunities.

The hospital room, once a battleground of pain and fear, transformed into a sacred space where a new chapter of my life was written. Gazing upon my son, I realized this was more than the birth of a child; it was the rebirth of my soul, healed and made whole.

In that serene room, with my newborn son nestled against me, I embraced the dawning of a new era - an era of love, healing, and boundless possibilities. It was a poignant realization that no matter where life had taken me, the future was a canvas of hope, ready to be painted with the vibrant hues of love and life. This moment marked not an end, but a beautiful beginning.

Returning home with our baby marked the start of a new world, one teeming with profound joy and a sense of awe-inspiring responsibility. The car ride was a quiet journey, filled with the soft, rhythmic breathing of our baby and a shared, unspoken understanding of our transformed lives.

Once home, the reality of our new roles enveloped us. Holding my son in the nursery, a sanctuary we had lovingly prepared, I was struck by a blend of admiration and anxiety. How could someone so tiny elicit such intense, complex emotions?

The initial nights were a whirlwind of feedings, diaper changes, and gentle soothes. Jake and I navigated these routines in a state of wonder, exhaustion, and profound love. Watching him cradle our son, his voice a soft melody, filled my heart with warmth and reinforced the deep bond we shared.

Despite the sleepless nights, each morning dawned with a sense of purpose and resolve. I dedicated myself to creating a nurturing environment for our son, a stark contrast to my own childhood experiences. Hours were spent holding him close, speaking words of love, and infusing his life with joy.

"Look at all these colors," I would coo during our playtimes, guiding his tiny hands over the vibrant pages of a picture book. His bright eyes followed each movement, his delighted gurgles filling the room.

The disparity between my own childhood and the life I was crafting for my son was profound. Where my early years were marred by fear and uncertainty, his were being sculpted with love and security. Watching him sleep peacefully in his crib, a deep sense of fulfillment enveloped me, knowing that I was actively breaking the cycle of my past.

As days melded into weeks, our home flourished with the sounds and sights of a happy, thriving child. Laughter echoed off the walls, and each room bore witness to the care and love we poured into our son's life. Books, toys, and images created an environment rich with love and safety.

One afternoon, as we lay on the floor, I pointed to a colorful image in a book. "And this is a lion," I explained, his tiny hand reaching out to explore the page. In his curious gaze, I saw the reflection of a world ripe with wonder and endless possibilities, a world we were eager to explore together.

Creating this nurturing environment extended beyond the physical; it encompassed the emotional atmosphere we fostered. Our home resonated with gentle lullabies, tender kisses, and a constant stream of encouragement. I nurtured not just his physical needs but his soul, infusing his life with the love and understanding I had longed for in my youth.

Each action, each choice, was a manifestation of the love and compassion I had craved as a teenager. My son would never question his worth; he would grow up feeling cherished, supported, and valued. Through him, I was healing my own past, forging a future anchored in love and security.

In the early dawn hours, when the world was still and hushed, I often found myself deep in thought. Holding my son in the soft glow of the nursery, I contemplated the path that had led me to this moment. From the shadowed valleys of a tumultuous past to the light of a hopeful future, my journey had been one of courage and transformation.

"Everything has changed, hasn't it?" I murmured to my son, his gentle breathing a soothing lullaby in the quiet room. "You've changed everything."

One afternoon, Jake found me lying on our bed, enveloped in introspection. He joined me, his presence a comforting embrace. "What's on your mind?" he inquired gently.

"I was just thinking about how far I've come," I responded, gazing into his eyes. "From a survivor to a protector. It's been an incredible journey."

Jake held my hand tenderly. "You're the most resilient person I know, Sarah. You've created a world of beauty and love for our son."

His words resonated deeply, bolstering my resolve. I had indeed transformed. Each day presented its own set of challenges, but in every interaction with my son, in every decision I faced, I tapped into a strength I had only recently discovered.

There were moments of doubt, times when the whispers of my past crept in, casting shadows of insecurity. Yet, I confronted them with a fierce love for my son. I was committed to providing him with a childhood enriched with love, a stark contrast to the one I had known. My love for him was a shield, safeguarding him and guiding his path.

Gazing at my son, a profound sense of gratitude washed over me. Here, in this moment, the narrative of my life reached its zenith. I had navigated a sea of adversities, but those trials had sculpted me into the person I was now – a mother, a protector, a beacon of hope.

This new chapter of my life was a testament to the transformative power of love. In loving my son, I was not only gifting him a life filled with joy but also rediscovering my own strength and capacity for unconditional love. Each day marked a step in a journey of healing and growth, a path tread by both my son and me.

This was our new horizon.

AUTHOR'S NOTE

As this novel comes to an end, I find it both an obligation and a privilege to share a bit of truth that lies at the heart of this story. While the characters and setting details within these pages are a product of fiction, their emotional journeys, struggles, and triumphs are deeply rooted in the true events of my own past. This novel is a story created from my personal experiences intertwined with the imaginative elements that give life to fiction.

Sarah's story is a vivid testament to the resilience of the human spirit. Through her, I have sought to portray the incredible capacity of an individual to rise from the ashes of despair, to confront and overcome seemingly unconquerable adversities. Sarah's journey is not just about the challenges she faces but also about the inner transformation that these challenges infuse.

In crafting this narrative, my deepest hope was to resonate with each reader in a unique and personal way. It is a story that celebrates the power of transformation and the boundless potential within each one of us to forge our paths toward happiness and fulfillment. It is a reminder that, regardless of the obstacles we face, our spirit remains invincible, and our ability to change and adapt is limitless.

As you step away from this novel, may you carry with you a profound appreciation for the journey of life, with all its twists and turns. May Sarah's story inspire you to believe in the possibility of brighter days, even in the darkest of times. Above all, may you always remember that within you lies an endless reservoir of strength, courage, and hope, ready to propel you towards your dreams.

Thank you for joining me on this journey. May it be a beacon of hope and a source of inspiration as you navigate the chapters of your own life story.

With heartfelt gratitude,

Jenny Houghton Thomas

ABOUT THE AUTHOR

Jenny Houghton Thomas, an entrepreneur and debut author, brings a wealth of personal and professional experience to her psychological drama for young adults. Her own journey, having grown up in the foster care system, infuses her writing with authenticity and profound insight. Her novel explores the nuanced story of a young girl's path through trauma and resilience, mirroring the complexities Jenny navigated in her youth. Balancing her entrepreneurial spirit with her role as a mother to five children, supported by her husband Daniel, Jenny's family life enriches her storytelling. Her home, always bustling with the activities of her children and the companionship of five dogs and a cat, serves as a constant source of inspiration and joy. Jenny's writing is not just a reflection of her imaginative prowess; it's a testament to her resilience and ability to connect with readers, especially those facing their own challenges. Her upbringing in the foster care system lends a unique depth and empathy to her narrative. Join her in discovering stories that resonate with courage, hope, and the triumph of the human spirit.

www.ingramcontent.com/pod-product-compliance
Lightning Source LLC
Chambersburg PA
CBHW021142310726
48971CB00002B/451